ASSUMED NAME

ASSUMED NAME

by

Ricardo Piglia

Translated by

Sergio Gabriel Waisman

Latin American Literary Review Press
Series: Discoveries
Pittsburgh, Pennsylvania
1995

The Latin American Literary Review Press publishes Latin American creative writing under the series title *Discoveries*, and critical works under the series title *Explorations*.

Library of Congress Cataloging-in-Publication Data

Piglia, Ricardo.
[Nombre falso. English]
Assumed name / by Ricardo Piglia; translated by Sergio Gabriel Waisman.
p. cm. -- (Discoveries)
Contents: Author's note--The end of the ride--Mousy Benítez sang boleros--The glass box--The madwoman and the story of the crime--The price of love--Assumed name--Homage to Roberto Arlt--Appendix, Luba.
ISBN 0-935480-71-4
I. Waisman, Sergio Gabriel. II. Arlt, Roberto, 1900-1942. Luba.
III. Title. IV. Series.
IN PROCESS
863--dc20   95-22340
                                        CIP

The paper used in this publication meets the minimum requirements of the American National Standard for Performance of Paper for Printed Library Materials Z39.48-1984. ∞

Assumed Name can be ordered directly from the publisher:

Latin American Literary Review Press
121 Edgewood Avenue • Pittsburgh, PA 15218
Tel(412)371-9023 • Fax(412)371-9025

Contents

Acknowledgments

This project is supported in part by grants from the National Endowment for the Arts in Washington D.C., a federal agency, and the Commonwealth of Pennsylvania Council on the Arts.

Translator's Acknowledgements

I would like to thank Professor Raymond Williams at the University of Colorado, Boulder for introducing me to Ricardo Piglia's work, and the following people for their support and encouragement: Sidney Goldfarb, Maureen Adams, Marta Waisman, and Eduardo Waisman.

Sergio Gabriel Waisman

Sergio Gabriel Waisman's translation of Ricardo Piglia's story "La loca y el relato del crimen" ("The Madwoman and the Story of the Crime") was first published in *Chelsea 58*.

Introduction

Sergio Gabriel Waisman

Ricardo Piglia has been hailed as one of the most accomplished Latin American writers of his generation. Born in 1940 in Adrogué, in the Province of Buenos Aires, Argentina, he is the author of five books of fiction and numerous critical essays. *Assumed Name (Nombre falso)* is the book that first established Piglia's international importance with striking singularity. The five stories, and the novella after which the collection takes its name, caught the attention of critics and readers soon after its publication in 1975 in Buenos Aires. *Assumed Name* is presented here for the first time in English; it has already been translated into French and Portuguese.

Assumed Name is Ricardo Piglia's second collection of stories. He published a previous collection in 1967 entitled *La invasión*; it received a prestigious award from the Casa de las Américas and was republished in Cuba as *Jaulario*. After *Assumed Name*, he published his first novel, *Artificial Respiration (Respiración artificial)*, in 1980. Duke University Press' English translation of *Artificial Respiration* was released in 1994. It has been called one of the most important novels to come out of Latin America in recent decades. Since then, he has also published *Crítica y ficción*, a compilation of interviews and essays on the poetics of narrative, in 1986; *Prisión perpetua,* encompassing twenty years of Piglia's short fiction, in 1988; and his second novel, *Ciudad ausente*, in 1992.

Introducing a book that is so much about the country in which it is written, that is so ingrained with issues of that country's identity and its literary canon, is a difficult task. Readers familiar with Argentina, with its politics, its history, and/or its literature, might find such an introduction superfluous. For those unfamiliar with Argentina, the book will, in all likelihood, serve as its own introduction. All readers, however, will discover an entire country in the five short stories and the novella which comprise *Assumed Name*.

The background for the five short stories in *Assumed Name* is the Argentina of the 1950s, '60s, and '70s—a country wrought with sociopolitical unrest, punctuated by military takeovers. Since 1943, the military has handpicked thirteen of Argentina's twenty-two presidents. The protagonists of these stories inherit their past; they live in it even as it becomes the present and the future. It is as if these marginalized characters, always seeking to engage—themselves, each other—echo a society that has lived virtually on the brink, socially and psychologically, for the better part of this century. In an environment of violence and death, the characters' search for meaning, for direction, is glimpsed only along the outskirts of their lives: a conversation on an all-night train ride, a newspaper clipping, a gesture between two men, a diary entry, a girl's song: fragments that *must* somehow form a whole.

A major aspect of any country's identity is its literary inheritance; particularly, how that inheritance is viewed in the present. Argentina's literary lineage, as complex as any in the hemisphere, is ingeniously explored in the novella "Assumed Name." Ricardo Piglia draws from what is usually considered the two polar opposites of modern Argentine literature: Roberto Arlt's urban novels and Jorge Luis Borges' literary labyrinths. In the process, Argentina's literary heritage seems put to the test. "Assumed Name" falls partially under a kind of "detective thriller" genre, as the reader follows Piglia step by step in his search for a missing manuscript. With its many literary and historical allusions, "Assumed Name" also doubles, at times, as literary criticism. Borges' work from the 1940s resonates in these literary devices. But here, in Ricardo Piglia's unique creation, the subject of the search is, paradoxically enough, a previously unpublished short story allegedly belonging to Roberto Arlt.

When he was asked to discuss these issues in a 1986 interview published in *Hispamerica: Revista de Literatura*, Piglia said:

> *Crossing Arlt with Borges, to use a positivistic metaphor, is one of the great utopias of Argentine literature. I think that this temptation is present, more or less consciously, in Onetti, in Cortázar, and in Marechal. Arlt and Borges are the two great Argentine writers; and, in a certain sense, all of the genealogies, all of the relationships and all of the intrigues of contemporary Argentine literature arises from them.*

The relationship between art and money, between truth and fiction, arise along the way. The enigmatic tale of "Nombre Falso" does not attempt to formulate the *answers* to the historical and literary questions of our times; rather, it does something far more difficult, and far more unusual: it formulates the *questions* necessary to begin a discussion about a national literary identity.

The only things that we lose are those that we never really had.

ROBERTO ARLT

Author's Note

I wrote the stories in this book (except for one) in 1975. At that time, I lived in an apartment in Buenos Aires on Sarmiento, in front of the old market on Montevideo, and when I think about these stories I remember a window that faced a patio. I suppose that the fact of having written them while looking from time to time at the light from that window gives them a certain unity for me: as if the stories had been there, on the other side of the glass.

That year a popular magazine organized a contest of detective stories with an unusual prize: two tickets to Paris and a paid, fifteen-day stay in a first-class hotel. I thought the affair so extravagant, and the judging committee so heterogeneous (Borges, Roa Bastos and Denevi), that I decided to write a story. The result was "The Madwoman and the Story of the Crime," with which I won first prize; thus, I went to Paris and stayed a spell at the Hotel Méridien. Actually, it was the trip that really obeyed the rules of the detective genre. The situation was so strange that the whole time I felt like a kind of counterfeiter who was going to be discovered at any moment. On the other hand, I confirmed that writing by assignment, starting with certain set rules, produces a paradoxical feeling of freedom. Stravinsky affirmed that restrictions and limits were the condition that his music required. "Otherwise," he said, "the moment I sit down to compose

I find myself overwhelmed by the infinite possibilities." I was not able to include "The Madwoman and the Story of the Crime" in the first edition of *Nombre falso*; I substituted it with "The Trial Record" ("Las actas del juicio"), a story from a previous book. In the current edition I have rearranged the collection according to the original order.

The only autobiographical aspect of "The End of the Ride" is the journey in which the events occur: one night I was traveling by bus from Mar del Plata and a woman committed suicide in the bathroom of some forgotten stop along the road. It is another person—a man—who commits suicide in the story, and another woman who is encountered, but the experience is the same. "Mousy Benítez Sang Boleros" is from 1968. It formed part of a collection which I wrote after publishing *La invasión*; I included it in *Assumed Name* because its style was different from the stories that I had always written. A writer whom I admire made me see that "The Glass Box" was a variation on the theme of the double. After he said it, it seemed evident to me, but I did not think of that while I wrote it. For years I had tried to tell the story of a man who can prevent a death with one word but, from apathy or from wickedness, remains silent. The intrigue narrated in "The Price of Love" is essentially true. It was revealed to me, with sad irony, by the protagonist, from whom, to tell the truth, her friend stole a set of silver. We will never know why we decide that certain stories are ours and we can tell them, while others (often better ones), which we imagine or live, are another's and are lost. This is what, I believe, the novella—after which this book takes its name—is about. I started with the image of a certain Kostia who spent his life at the bar *Ramos* telling anecdotes about Roberto Arlt. The story slowly transformed into what it is now. I am sure that it is the best thing I have written. Perhaps I think this because I wrote it with the certainty that for the first time I had managed to perceive what was truly to be seen on the other side of the window.

R. P.
Buenos Aires, August 31, 1994

THE END OF THE RIDE

1

Lost in the lobby of the half-empty station, Emilio Renzi watches the poorly illuminated platforms, the yellowish light that fades into darkness. Frail, aged, he is dressed in a black coat that makes him look pale, accentuating his irritable and absent-minded appearance. It is fifteen minutes before the departure of the bus; behind the fogged windows the trees of Plaza Constitución dissolve in the mist. Everything is distant, vaguely unreal, as if he had always been in that lobby waiting to travel, as if it had been years since he had received the call. He would be arriving the following morning; until then, there was nothing to do but wait. Few traveled with him, nine or ten people crowded together in front of a wooden bar that separated them from the platform. They had the livid and anxious faces of those who go to Mar del Plata in winter, out of season, on casino days. They gave the impression of knowing one another, or of sharing some secret, and they greeted each other from afar, with the look of accomplices. To one side, near the desk where the luggage was checked in, a tall, red-haired woman wrapped in a fur coat seemed to be arguing with a mild and elegant man who wore a hat and a fine mustache. "It will never be the same," Emilio heard the woman say with a painful, brittle voice. "Never, ever will it be the same," she said, and it looked like the quiet man threatened her or apologized to her, restrained. The sour music that came from the speakers mixed and clashed with the rumbling of the city. The night was cold; a cold, windy night. Emilio walked along the platform to the beach where the empty buses were kept; the place smelled of gasoline and humidity; black and yellow stripes shone on the poorly-painted walls as if buried under the iron arches that framed the ceiling. "It is useless to look for explanations," Emilio thought. "Perhaps it's already too late." At the newspaper he had said that his father was seriously ill. "He had an accident," he told Laurenz. "They informed me on the phone; I'm traveling tonight." He did not want to say more: everything seemed to be false and without reason.

He waited until the others got on the bus, then entered. His seat was in the center of the car. He walked along the rubber-carpeted aisle, passing in profile between those who were finishing taking their seats, and arranged himself next to the window. Outside, the fog was a bluish mist that covered the city. The red-haired woman sat to his right on the other side of the aisle. The man who had been with her stayed behind, standing alone on the deserted platform. The woman smoked without looking at him, withdrawn, a handbag resting on her knees. When the bus began to move, the man remained motionless, floating in the gray light, still and calm, saying goodbye with a hand raised in the emptiness.

Shortly afterward the station was left behind and they traveled slowly through the city, heading south. Emilio lit a cigarette and relaxed his body in his seat. The mist was turning into a dense and balmy rain. "It's going to rain all night," he thought, and felt calm for the first time, surrendering to the rumbling of the motion. He had received the call late in the afternoon; now the memory was remote and confused. "It is very grave," the woman told him hastily, crying. "I'm Elisa, a friend of your father's. He is checked in at the Yeres Clinic. He left a letter for you." Emilio remembered the house where his father lived alone, the ample library full of sun with the black leather armchairs, the curtains filled with wind. He had locked himself in that room. He himself had called for help; they found him sitting down, facing the window, breathing with difficulty but calm, trying to put bandages on himself to stop the blood. "No one imagined what he was going to do. Nobody," the woman said as if she were apologizing for herself. "Nobody. No one could have imagined."

For a while the bus had been running with the lights off; in the semi-darkness, Emilio watched the white headlights of the cars racing in the rain. "That was why he came the last time, to tell me, so that I'd know or help him," he thought. "He came for that, he came to tell me. He didn't have the courage for it, or he was not able to, or I didn't

realize it." It had always been the same: his father lied, tried to keep
his dignity, falsifying everything; he calmed others when it was he
who needed comforting. "I'm happy," he told him that night when
they said good-bye at the train station, the potent light of the locomotive exposing the darkness of the platform. He smoked ceaselessly,
his pinkish fingers stained by the pale tobacco, playing with the black
stone ring that he had always had. "Don't worry about me," he had
said with his transparent voice, cracking from the cigarette, and right
away he hugged him as if he did not want to hear him. Emilio watched
him leave, standing tall, turning his face around to say good-bye with
a timid, brief smile. That was the last time they saw each other. His
father had arrived unexpectedly that afternoon, without announcing
himself. Emilio was surprised by his clear voice coming in through
the window in the room facing the inner patio. He was asking for him
in another apartment, as if he had gotten lost, surly, resolute, certain
of not being wrong. He kept listening to that obstinate tone; when at
last he went into the hallway, he saw him at the landing of the stairs,
a man who looked older than he was, dressed in an elegance that was
out of style, climbing wearily. "Where have you come to live?" he had
said, talking quickly as he always did when he was moved. He wore
a double-breasted suit, an old-fashioned fit, and a blue tie over his
slightly frayed, white shirt. He avoided looking straight at him with
his clear eyes, but he seemed happy. He made fantastic plans, the same
as always, letting himself get carried away by the words, as if his son
were a stranger and he wanted to win him over. At any rate, only
toward the end of the evening, in a restaurant on Carlos Pellegrini, did
Emilio believe he understood the reason for that trip. They were
finishing dinner and all of a sudden his father started talking to him in
a bold and cloudy manner about a woman. Enthusiastic, self-assured
and cheerful, he confined himself in a virile and slightly dirty complic-
ity to speak about her, and he finally became obstinate that Emilio go
with him to meet her. The woman lived in a newly occupied
apartment; suitcases and open trunks were scattered about the floor,
which was covered with newspapers, and there was no furniture other
than the double bed with a metal headboard. The three of them sat on
that bed and his father was satisfied, as if in reality he had traveled
there to have him meet that pale woman with dark circles under her

eyes who acquiesced in a humble manner without speaking. Her name was Elvira; she served a sweet, orange-tasting liqueur that his father did nothing but praise. When they were leaving the woman held his father back, and Emilio went near the window to leave them alone; he watched the soft lights of the city burning below and heard them speak nervously in a low voice. "Why, Juan José? No. But my heart is breaking. I never said that," she was saying, and his father was calming her down. When they said good-bye it seemed to him that the woman had cried, her eyes were moist and she was flushed. In the elevator his father fixed his clothes facing the mirror and cleaned his mouth with a white handkerchief, as if he wanted him to see that the woman had kissed him.

The bus ran now with the lights on, at a low speed. It was nearly two in the morning, it had stopped raining. Shortly they came to a stop in the road. The place was sad, a long dance hall with mica-covered windows, painted light blue, and empty. Emilio sat down at a table close to the counter and ordered a gin. The people tending bar slid around slowly, half-asleep, with bored expressions. To one side the red-haired woman was putting coins into an automatic Victrola; she was listening to the music, standing alone with a glass in her hand, the bag resting on the floor, as if she had gotten out to stay. Emilio opened a black notebook, leaned on the table, and began to write: *Friday 17: On route to Mar del Plata. At mid afternoon they inform me on the telephone. I remember two things: that strange apparition, the last time, his voice coming from somewhere asking for me, disconcerted, as if he had lost me. The afternoon that we had a picture taken, the two of us, at the beach: he was fixing his hair that was falling on his forehead, he took off his glasses, and he placed his hand on my shoulder. I remember most of all the gesture of him fixing his hair and the mark of the glasses on the skin of his face, like a scar.* He finished his gin and lit a cigarette. The woman kept listening to the music, her back to him, a hand resting on the circular top of the Victrola. *I have always thought*, Emilio wrote, *that he was less vulnerable than I: the tenderness from man to man must be veiled. However, perhaps it's already too late. I admired him (I loved him) because he knew how to conceal his feelings. Now I have begun to write about him.* He saw the silhouette of the bus in the fogged window. The rumbling of the cars mixed with the soft music to which the woman was listening. *A woman listens to music, alone, illuminated by the bluish light of an ancient Victrola with a rounded top. She has a softly perverse appearance, her hair red. In Buenos Aires a man with cynical manners who remained alone on the platform saw her off, saying good-bye with a hand raised in the emptiness. It rains from time to time, it is two in the morning. I have begun to write about him in the past, as if he had already died.* He read over what he had written and put the notebook away. He called the waiter and paid. Then he walked toward the bathroom. He passed near the woman and heard her humming in a low voice, engrossed in the music. The bathroom walls were corroded by the humidity. One single lamp, placed in a gap near the ceiling, emitted a grayish light. Emilio turned on the faucet and looked at himself in the fogged mirror: his face seemed worn out, a decayed mask.

2

When he returned to the bar the woman was already gone, but the Victrola still played and the music filled the empty place. He did not see her when he got into the bus. She finally showed up, at the moment in which they were leaving, hurried, balancing on her high heels, the bag in her right hand. Emilio watched her settle into her seat and smoke facing the window; her face was reflected in the dark glass, illuminated from time to time by the cigarette's embers as they burned in the semi-darkness. Emilio reclined his seat back and tried to sleep. If everything went well they would arrive at seven in the morning. Julia must have looked for him the entire night, they had a date to have dinner together, but he had decided not to tell her that he was leaving. Perhaps she had called the newspaper; in any case, he could call her from Mar del Plata. The even humming of the engine made him drowsy; he remembered again the picture with his father at the beach, without being able to determine the year. Before he fell asleep he remembered that at that time the two of them still lived together. He dreamt that he was walking through a market where wool clothing was sold. It was nighttime and the place was illuminated by kerosene lamps. Emilio wore a felt hat that covered his eyes. Suddenly, on a dirt path, he found the olive colored coupé that his father had sold when his mother died. It was abandoned at a crossroads. Two women were in the front seat, the wind was striking one of the doors against the mudguard with a heavy sound. One of the women was leaning her face toward him and was speaking to him, smiling: "Come closer. Don't tell me you have forgotten me. All we used to do was talk about you." When he tried to get closer, he felt something like a pull, and woke up. The red-haired woman was standing, bent over him, and was shaking his arm softly.

"Is something the matter?" she said.

In the greenish semi-darkness the woman was a transparent silhouette, shining, pallid.

"You were talking out loud, you were complaining. I thought you were suffering," she said with her strange and somehow perforated voice.

"I was talking," Emilio said, confused, without detaching himself completely from the dream. "I dreamt something, I don't know."

"That was it. I thought something was wrong. Excuse me, then."

"On the contrary, no, I thank you," he said. The woman was still standing, ample and quiet in the aisle. "Won't you sit down, please?" Emilio said, and smiled at her. "I wouldn't want to fall asleep again."

"I can never sleep when I travel," the woman said, smiling slightly, as if there were something behind him, on the other side of the window, that made her cheerful. "I hate to travel. There is nothing to do but think."

She sat down softly, gracefully shifting her ample and beautiful body, which emitted a sweet perfume like that of dead flowers.

"I saw you in the bar," he said. "You were listening to music."

"Music?" she said, and let out the laughter that she had been foreshadowing. "Noise, you should say, rather. I can't stand those places, they're so sad."

Emilio offered her cigarettes; he could see her better in the bluish glow of the flame: she had a doll-like, amiable face; the skin, refined and taut, a frail, rosy color.

"It's strange," she said all of a sudden. "I'm sure we've seen each other before, you and I."

"It could be," he said.

"Do you travel often?"

"Yes," he said. "My father lives in Mar del Plata."

"Bad city to live in. People go there to gamble, to get sun, how could anyone live there?"

"Like every place," he said. "You get used to it."

The woman looked straight at him now, always sitting sideways, her legs crossed, smoking with placid movements.

"I know where we've seen each other. One night, it must be two months ago: you were in the casino, on a streak, winning nonstop. It was unbelievable, I never saw anyone win like you did that night. Do you always have such luck?"

"She uses this trick," he thought, "she could have chosen any other."

"Sometimes," he said.

"But then, why do you complain in your sleep?"

"Who can tell. Just like if I were to ask you why you were arguing with that man who was with you at the station."

"You heard me," she said, and smiled, as if this made her happy. "I was not arguing, no. I would never be able to argue with him. He asked me to stay, that was all. He's good, too good. He doesn't want me to go to the casino. Those who don't gamble can't understand. Isn't that how it is?"

"Yes," he said.

"Everything is so boring. I believe that if I weren't able to go to the casino I'd go crazy. One goes and gambles, one knows that one is going to lose, but that doesn't matter at all. When I'm gambling I forget everything. I forget who I am, the money, I forget everything and I'm another woman. I don't know, it's hard to explain," she said, a peaceful calmness on her tender and childlike face. "What line of work are you in?"

"I'm a journalist."

"A journalist? How marvelous. Don't tell me that you cover

crime."

"No," he said. "Unfortunately, I only do book reviews."

"That's a shame," she said, amused. "It would be fascinating if, for example, you were going to Mar del Plata to do a piece on some crime that had occurred. And what is it like doing book reviews?"

"A little monotonous," Emilio said. "And you, what line of work are you in?"

"Me? None. I haven't done anything for five years," she raised her head, searching for the clarity of the window, as if wanting him to see her always-cheerful eyes. "I was an opera singer, but five years ago I lost my voice. It seems absurd, doesn't it? I got up one morning and I couldn't sing anymore. Everybody thinks that I'm going to recover, but I know that it's impossible. Sometimes I dream that I'm healed, that I'm once again on stage. Perhaps that's why I had to wake you when I saw you complaining. I cannot resign myself to it. Music was my life."

"And how did you lose your voice?"

"Who knows? I was in Italy: I was to make a debut in the Scala, that night I had rehearsed Donizetti and I went to sleep happy as ever. It was summer. Suddenly I felt like I was drowning, and when I woke up I couldn't sing anymore. It's very common. You pray every night that it won't happen, but there you have it."

In the lifeless air of the bus the woman's voice sounded low and harsh.

"You won't believe it, but I predicted it," she said after a silence. "So much time has passed and yet I remember that morning as if it were today: I went out to the window, crying, it was hard to breathe, everyone was with me, giving me breathing space. It was such a beautiful day, full of sun, and I thought: that's it, now it's already happened to me, now I am not afraid. It was as if I had always been waiting for that moment." She stayed still and lifted her face, which looked like it was made of glass; then she tried to smile. "I don't know why I have to talk about these things, they are so distant, it's as if another had lived them. May I have a cigarette?"

Emilio stretched the pack out to her and the woman leaned toward the flame, her hands together to protect the match.

"They don't let me smoke," she said. "Before I couldn't and

now they don't let me, it's fatal for the voice. But I don't care now, I know that I'll never be able to sing again."

At that moment the bus lights went on; the woman's figure dissolved in the smoke, as if wrapped in a veil.

"It's stopped raining," she said, and smiled at him, timidly, saddened, stretching a gloved hand out to him. "My name is Aída Monti."

3

The bus had come to another stop along the road. Emilio and the woman drank coffee at a table near the window. She smoked in silence, her imitation leather suitcase resting on the greasy floor. The two seemed to float behind a dirty glass, covered by the yellowish lamps that illuminated the bar.

"You don't believe me," the woman said.

"Yes, I believe you. Why wouldn't I believe you?"

"Certainly you don't believe me, and it's a shame."

She bent over smoothly to open the suitcase; Emilio saw her move her hands among the dresses and the white clothes. When she raised her head she looked like another woman.

"This is me," she said, handing him a photograph.

The woman had braided hair, a headband across her forehead, dressed like a Valkyrie, in profile on an empty stage. The picture was blurry, poorly lit; there was something artificial in the scenery, it seemed to have been taken in a studio, against a painted curtain where you could see clouds, angels, and the sun's rays vacillating in the blue sky.

"Beautiful," he said. "You look beautiful. But the picture wasn't necessary. I don't understand what makes you think that I won't believe you."

"You are right if you doubt me, a woman who travels alone, who speaks with a man she barely knows, underneath it all you must think that I'm half crazy."

"No," he said. "No."

"Oh, I know," she said, taking the picture with both hands. "Do you like it? It's such a long time ago. I'm in Belgium, doing Wagner." She moved the picture away from her face, as if it were a mirror. "Do you have something to write with?"

Emilio handed her a pen and watched her bend over, studiously, and write on the back of the picture, flipped over on the table.

"Here," she said, finally. "Save it as a souvenir."

Emilio took the glossy cardboard and read in the humid clarity: *For Emilio Renzi who complains in his sleep, with friendship from Aída Monti. April of 1970.*

"It's not anything," she interrupted him when he began to thank her. "We better go, it's time already."

They walked slowly toward the bus under the bar's awning. The light illuminated the trees, the graveled path that ended in darkness.

"It must be strange to live in a place like this," she said, and took him by the arm, the bag in her left hand. "To see all those people arrive and leave. To work at night, waiting for the buses to arrive."

"Yes," he said. "But one can become accustomed even to this."

They got on again and sat together. The bus maneuvered in the macadam and out to the road, under the rain. As they gained speed the heating fogged up the air, a tenuous vapor layering against the windows. The rubber blades of the windshield wipers swept away the water, breaking the headlights of the cars that passed in front of them. The woman had taken off her coat; she wore a low-cut, blue silk dress that whitened her skin.

"Tell me something," she said suddenly, pressing her body against Emilio's.

"What can I tell you?"

"I don't know. Any story. The time you won or the time you lost."

Emilio hugged her and leaned over to kiss her.

"No," she said, gently, holding him back.

"Why?"

"I know. It's better not to."

She moved slightly and rested her head against Emilio's

shoulder, soft, docile.

"I hope it rains the whole ride," she said, as if to herself, with her eyes closed, an expression of stillness on her childlike face. The bus now ran at a sustained velocity, engulfed in a soft hum. The trees were blurry stains on the other side of the windows. Emilio felt the warm weight of the woman against his body and tried not to move. "She sleeps or pretends to sleep," he thought. "She smells like grass, like a recently bathed baby. She lies like others cry or complain." He remembered the picture, the leather strips of the sandals braided above the ankle, the concentrated manner in which she raised her arms, as if she were praying. He imagined the provincial theaters, the woman singing Verdi arias poorly, enthusiastically, accompanied on the piano by the man with the fine mustache. He heard her weak breathing, a hand on her chest, her hair covering her eyes. Without meaning to he thought of his father on the landing of the stairs that afternoon, disoriented and aged, his sweet eyes behind his glasses. A disenchanted man, ironical, who watched himself live—timid and confused when he spoke about himself. Almost without sound, on the roof of the bus but with a sense of distance, the rain continued in the middle of the night. "We are floating smoothly and quickly. I don't have to think," Emilio thought. "There's no reason why I should blame myself. He left a letter for me. It's like a dream and the woman is crazy. I could tell her that I'm not asking for anything other than to not be alone tonight, for her to say a word for me, because I don't want to be alone and she knows it, the crazy woman, dressed up like a Valkyrie, her cat-like voice, her swollen, doll-like face, to keep me company, her skin warm and perfumed." The cars honking broke up the mist and the sky cleared up in the middle of the rain. "Not to arrive, to continue traveling, to see him later, sitting in the wicker chair, in front of the mirror. A sad man, always willing to believe in others more than himself," he thought. "There's nothing else," Emilio thought and moved barely to look for the cigarettes. At that moment the woman woke up, calm, her cotton face framed by the curls of red hair.

"Have we arrived?" she asked.

"We don't have long to go."

"I was able to sleep. It's unbelievable. It's nearly six already.

My face must look like something else. Hold on, I'll fix myself up a little," she said, and set the bag on her lap. "She doesn't use a purse," he thought. "Everything she has in the world she must take in there: jars, handkerchiefs, cream, white clothes, pictures of herself singing Wagner for her family, dressed up like a Valkyrie, phony pictures taken by the guy who went to see her off at the station." He watched her hold up her hair at the nape of her neck, both arms raised above her head, the bobby pins between her teeth. Her face looked fresh and clean, framed by her red hair, her bare neck was smooth and very white, incredibly fragile. "As if she had conserved the neck of a girl, the throat she had as a youth, while her body gained weight."

"How long will you be staying in Mar del Plata?" she said, looking in her little hand-held mirror at her just-painted lips.

"I don't know," he said. "It depends."

The day had dawned suddenly, and a weak clarity filtered through the clouds. At a distance, whiter than the white of daybreak, the outline of the city began to take form.

"There are three casino days," she said. "I'm sure I'll go back Monday or Sunday night."

"That's good," he said. "Let's hope you win."

"Me? No. I'm a woman with bad luck."

They passed by a park with thin trees and pebbled flower beds. Toward the rear, a serene fog appeared which seemed to blend into the horizon.

"There's the sea," the woman said with her face right up against the window.

When they entered the terminal it was seven in the morning. It was sprinkling lightly; on the platform the air was frozen and still.

"It's going to keep raining," she said as they crossed the empty station. "Will we see each other later?"

"I won't be able to," he said.

"Why? I'll give you my address. It's so damn cold here. Do you have something to write on?"

They had stopped at the foot of a staircase, in front of the lobby's glass door. In the street a bright sign traced blue circles, unevenly. Emilio searched in the pocket of his coat and handed her the picture.

"Write here," he said to her.

She wrote, once again carefully and studiously, leaning against the glass door.

"I'm going to be here. If you come we'll go to the casino together."

"I don't think I'll be able to."

The woman closed the top of her coat with both hands.

"That's too bad," she said, and smiled at him. "I was sure you'd bring me luck." With a quick gesture she leaned toward him and touched his face lightly with her lips. "Okay, good-bye then."

Emilio held her by the arm, gentle and firm.

"Just one thing," he said. "Why do you lie?"

She moved slightly and looked at his face.

"So I don't get bored when I travel," she said, and pushed the glass door with her body.

4

The clinic was in a flat building, an old fashioned construction, buried behind a garden of deserted flower beds. Emilio went up in an elevator with aluminum walls that climbed slowly. His father's room was at the end of a hallway that smelled of ether and bleach disinfectant. A nurse with a large-boned face and jumpy eyes approached, swaying heavily as she walked.

"Mister Renzi? Are you the son? Come," she said. "This way."

"I want to speak with the doctor."

"The doctor will be back later. We have to wait. Nothing has been determined yet." She spoke with a kind of low hiss, and Emilio had to make an effort to understand her. "Come, there is a lady waiting for you to arrive." There was a slight contempt in the manner in which she referred to her, and Emilio was able to imagine his father's friend even before he saw her get up from the leather chair and stretch out the hem of her skirt as she crossed the small room, with its low ceiling and cretonne curtains, toward him.

"I'm Elisa," the woman said. "You're Emilio, right? We spoke on the phone."

The woman had a hardened, boyish face, tarnished by tears or fatigue; a face that was defenseless behind the violent red of the poorly painted lips.

"Yes," he said, without smiling; she stopped without finishing the gesture of going near him to greet him.

"Go in for just one moment," the nurse said. "And try not to talk much."

"Go," the woman said. "He's waiting for you."

When he entered, blinded, he only managed to see the white bulk of the bed and a bluish glow that came from a lamp veiled by a handkerchief. It was very hot inside. His father was lying face up and breathing with an anguished gasping, his lips flayed by fever.

"You've arrived," he said.

Emilio went to him and felt along the rough material of the bedspread until he found his father's hand, frozen, brittle, as if it were made of paper.

"See how I am," his father said with a muffled voice, trying to smile.

"Don't speak Dad, rest," Emilio said.

"This is all so ridiculous," his father said. "So ridiculous, shit! God!"

His eyes became cloudy, glassy upon the ashen oval of his thinned face.

"Everything is going to be okay," Emilio said.

"Sure," his father said. "Everything is going to be okay."

Emilio felt his body soften, a burning in his bones. "I'm here," he thought. "I'm with him."

"I left you a letter," his father said.

"It's okay," he said. "Don't worry."

"Tear it up. Don't read it," his father said.

"Don't worry," Emilio said.

He tried to think of something else to say, but he couldn't. A hushed rumbling came from the other side of the window shutters, similar to an automobile's engine. His father had closed his eyes. Emilio saw his fevered face as if from very far away, as if he were submerged in water. The nurse entered with a silver box; she went to the table and turned on the overhead light. In the sickly clarity his father was an even weaker and more fragile figure. Through the neckline of the pajama, he could see his gray hair, sparse on his sunken chest. The nurse leaned over the bed.

"Does it still hurt?" she said. His father looked at her without answering. "It will pass soon. I'm going to give you a sedative now." She opened the injections box and raised a syringe against the light. "You have to leave," she said, without looking at Emilio. "So he can sleep."

Emilio thought that the woman spoke about his father as if he were not there, or as if he did not understand, with the benevolent and foolish tone that is used with children and drunks.

"I'll be outside," he said. "Stay calm."

His father smiled with much effort, trying to look self-assured and to not be afraid.

"You too," he said, and moved his right hand slowly, without separating his wrist from the bed, in a weak wave, his face lined and gray, tense against the tall pillows.

Emilio walked to the end of the hallway under the blinding morning light that glowed white upon the tiles. In the waiting room, the woman stood in profile against the window; she turned around when she heard him enter.

"Were you able to speak with him?"

"Barely," Emilio said. "It's better not…"

"Yes, of course," she said.

She sat on a chair near a low table; Emilio could not see her very well, half-blocked by a porcelain vase, as if broken into pieces by the paper flowers that blurred her face. The woman wore a party dress, with narrow laces and ruffles, yellowish on the edges, and wrinkled as if she always slept with that dress on.

"How can one explain these things?" she said. "He seemed so happy. He came to take me out to eat, and then all of a sudden he wanted to leave, to be alone. He locked himself in, no one heard anything." The woman interrupted herself, her eyes opaque. "He left this letter for you."

Emilio put the white, unopened envelope away in his coat

pocket.

"How could one know," she said. "You know how he is, always cheerful, always making plans. He never talks about how he's doing, he never says. How could I have imagined?" She was stretching the cuffs of her dress, the old, worn out lace edgings, until they covered the top of her hand. "The only thing was, once, a short time ago, I found a gun in a drawer. I became so frightened and then he told me that he had it for when he started becoming pitiable; he said it playfully, as if a gun were something that…. Sometimes I think that I should have realized. He was always so alone." The woman stopped talking, the blackened tips of her yellowish hair getting in her face. "In any case, even if I had realized it, what would I have done?"

"Nothing," Emilio said. "Don't worry."

"That's how he is. Ever since I have known him, that's how he is," she said. "You must know, always alone, always thinking to himself, laughing at God and the very Holy Mary."

"Yes," Emilio said. "Don't worry."

"I, you know, I love him very much," the woman said, and started crying softly. "Because sometimes one, when a man…," the woman said, distressed.

"Don't worry," Emilio said. "Why don't you go get some rest?"

"Okay," she said. "You're right."

She got up, shaking her velvet, lilac-colored, worn out and tidy dress, which came halfway up her leg, and looked at Emilio, insecure, grateful.

"I'll be back in the afternoon," she said. "I'll sleep a little."

"Yes," he said. "Go, don't worry."

The woman went up to him awkwardly and got up on her toes to kiss him on the cheek.

"Good-bye," she said. "Forgive me, I'm so nervous."

A clean and youthful expression whitened her face, as if she had conserved, in spite of everything, a certain childlike and obstinate confidence in her eyes. "She too," Emilio thought as he watched her leave. "She too, like the other: a docile woman, ridiculous, faithful. She too." He felt slightly dizzy, his body soft. "Nothing is going to happen," he forced himself to think. "There cannot be anything worse than this." He lit a cigarette and remained quiet for a while, smoking. When the curtains moved, filled with wind, he could see the oval arch of a closed doorway which faded into a gray wall. "It looks like a jail," he thought.

At that moment the nurse came out of his father's room.

"I'd like to go down for breakfast," Emilio said. "Where can I go?"

"Right across from the clinic there's a cafe," the woman said. "Go, don't worry, he'll sleep now."

The cafe was large and very well lit. Sitting in front of a window with aluminum shutters, his face turned toward the storm that clouded the morning, Emilio thought everything would dissolve in that rain: his father's pain, the clear eyes of the woman with the party dress. "Everything will be left clean and new," he thought.

He ordered sandwiches and a large coffee. The coffee was hot and very strong. He drank it without sugar, without letting it cool, and he felt better. The cafe was nearly empty. An old man, sitting on a tall stool at the counter, drank gin and smoked, studying the program for the races. Emilio lit a cigarette and looked for the black notebook in the pocket of his coat. He opened it without choosing: the pages were covered with uneven and tightly-packed handwriting. *Monday 12. If it's true that one must adapt to one's opposite*, he read at random, *if that is the "rule of life," this is due to the fact that we feel an instinctive horror to join together with he who expresses our same defects, our "way of being," etc. The reason being, evidently, that those same defects, that same mentality, discovered in he who lives with one, takes away from our illusion—which we had previously cultivated—that there exists a nucleus, let's say, in us, "original," different. All of this because of my meeting today with Julia. (Remember: while she explained her suffering to me, the pain in her soul, and she reproached me because it is known that I, etc., etc., she had time to study her face in the mirror, happy to look so beautiful. Is it not the same seduction that I feel for poses?: the skeptic, the dandy.)* He turned the pages until he reached a blank sheet; covering the first lines he found what he had written last night: *It rains from time to time, it is two in the morning. I have begun to write about him in the past, as if he had already died*, he read now. He left a space and began to write: *Saturday 18. It's nine in the morning. I'm in a cafe across from the clinic. Three months are enough to dissolve a man. What is left of him since the last time I saw him? A ghost who tries, always, to maintain his dignity. The most sinister thing is the vitreous sound of his breathing: one can hear his perforated lungs. Nobody with him: only that ruined woman wearing the party dress who looks like she just came out of a dance club. They're the best, he would say, as if it were enough, like always, for him to receive that indiscriminate and primitive tenderness. (And I?: on the trip, a desolate and fictitious Valkyrie. I quickly learn the best from my father.)* He lifted his face and saw, on the other side of the window, the figure of a young woman who walked sticking to the wall, her head curved down into her chest, pushing against the wind which made her umbrella shudder. *From here I can see the clinic's entrance,* he wrote now, *the distant and silent movement of the automobiles as they cross the avenue under the rain. Thinking consoles everything? I don't know. I would like to sleep six months, hibernate in a narcotic stupor: awake with my memory clean from all accusation, free forever from the eyes of criminals, of murdered ones. (Rhetoric. Wagner operas.) The bullet has grazed one of his lungs. I can only return and be with him to keep him company. Sad consolation.* He closed the notebook and put it away. Then he called the waiter. He was a man with an angular and mean face, with sad eyes. He had a defect in the joint of his right shoulder; he counted the money with just one hand, moving his fingers skillfully, the stiff arm on the table.

5

At the entrance to the clinic he felt the dry heat coming from the radiators. He went up in the elevator next to a woman cradling a baby that cried without solace. The woman covered it with a knitted blanket and patted its back softly with her fingertips.

When Emilio came out to the hallway it took him a while to understand that the open door was the one to his father's room. There was no one inside; the ceiling light was still on. The bed was unmade; the clothes rested on a metal chair. In the corridor, he saw a very young nurse approach, wearing a light-blue uniform.

"Where did you go? We've been looking for you," she said; Emilio felt a tug at his left side. "Your father had a hemorrhage, he's in the intensive care room."

"Where is it?"

"Come. I'll go with you."

They crossed a dark corridor, and, after going up some stairs, went into an ample lobby, illuminated by fluorescent tubes. Behind a glass wall, in a room with white walls, Emilio believed he saw his father, lying out on a stretcher between cloth screens.

"I'm going in," he said.

"It's not allowed."

"I'm going in, just the same."

The woman had a serene, distended expression.

"It's very grave," she said.

"I want to see him," he said.

"Come."

She went to a closet with beveled doors and handed him a hospital gown. Emilio stretched out his arms, and she adjusted the ties across his back; then she raised a surgical mask up to his face.

"Now you can enter," she said. "But only one moment, until the doctor returns."

In the room the light is white, everything seems to float in a soft haze. He feels strange with the surgical mask on his face and the hospital gown brushing lightly against his ankles. His father is at one end, laying down, a rubber tube covers his nose and his mouth: he breathes desperately, his forehead wet with perspiration, his cheekbones sunken. He watches with a cornered expression the nurse who every twenty seconds removes his mask, monitoring the oxygen pressure. Emilio gets close and searches for his father's face, but he does not look back, his eyes fixed on the woman's hand.

"I can't take it any more," his father says with a muffled voice.

Emilio forces himself to keep looking at that emaciated figure shivering between the sheets. "It's him," he thought. "It's him, it's my father."

"I can't take it any more," Emilio heard.

"Yes," the woman says. "Yes," she says, and connects the

valve. Emilio listens to the stifled whistling of the air going through the rubber tubes. "Come on, breathe," the nurse says, pressing on his father's chest with both hands.

Emilio hears a crackling sound, turbid like a vacuum valve, and immediately a silence, and immediately a noise similar to cloth tearing. His father breathes now using force, the tendons in his throat rigid under the cracked skin.

"You can't stay here," the nurse says. "Go. There's the doctor."

Emilio moves slowly, without looking at the stretcher. The doctor is near the door. He has both hands raised and someone puts a pair of latex gloves on them.

"Your father has had another hemorrhage," he says. "It's very grave."

"What can I do?" Emilio says, surprised by the false tone of his own voice.

"Nothing," the doctor says. "Wait."

Before leaving Emilio turns around; his father is a blurry image, his face deformed by the mask, his body like an arch on the stretcher. "It's a hemorrhage. A hemorrhage. The blood does not allow him to breathe."

Emilio took off the hospital gown and went toward the window. It was ten o'clock. He tried to stay calm and not think. Below, a nun in her habit crossed the patio pushing a two-wheeled cart full of white clothes into the wind. The invisible rumbling of the water gushing through the pipes could be heard in the walls. On the other side of the glass he saw the pale silhouette of the doctor and the aluminum crossbars of the stretcher on which his father lay. The nurses came in and out, passing in front of him. When he looked at the clock again it was nearly eleven. He buried his hands in his coat pockets and felt the texture of his father's letter, and further back, the glossy surface of the picture that the red-haired woman had given him. A heavy noise was heard from above, as if someone were dragging furniture. "A bed," he thought. "Someone is moving a bed." At that moment he saw the doctor start to walk toward the door, taking off his gloves. Emilio saw him come toward him, under the raw light, like in a dream. "He looks like a puppet," he thought. "A white puppet, without a face." The doctor pushed the swinging doors with his body. "We did everything possible," he said. "It was impossible to operate."

Emilio felt a metallic heaviness in his mouth and a feeling of abandon and of being cold. It seemed to him that the man's voice came from very far away.

"Don't stay here. You better wait below," the doctor, starting to walk toward the elevators, said.

Emilio remained alone in the lobby. Everything seemed to have stopped, coagulated in the warm air. On the other side of the glass wall was the stretcher with his father's body, a fragile and emaciated shadow, dissolving in the bitter light. They had covered his face with a white towel. "The Yeres Clinic. 441," Emilio read. "It's twelve," he thought. Two nurses passed by in front of him. "Does it pay on time?" one said. "I don't know. I wouldn't trust him if I were you," the other said. "It's already twelve," Emilio thought again, immobile in the middle of the empty room. "Now I have to go downstairs." He thought that he would not be able to move.

He heard voices at the landings of the stairs, muffled laughs that came from somewhere. When he reached the entrance lobby, the doctor was coming out of the elevator.

"You will have to go to Administration, Renzi," he told him. "You have to sign, you know."

"Yes," Emilio said.

The doctor had taken off his hospital gown and carried a coat on his arm. It was an old fashioned overcoat, with rounded lapels and nacre buttons.

"How old was your father?"

Emilio tried to remember.

"Fifty-five," he said randomly.

"You did everything possible," the doctor said.

"Yes," he said.

"On the first floor," the doctor said. "There is a desk at the end of the hallway."

"Okay," Emilio said. "First I'd like to go out to get something to drink."

"Don't worry. You did everything possible," the doctor said

again, leaving.

In the street the air is dirty, mixed with a turbid fog. On the sidewalk opposite they have turned on the lights of the cafe; a milky clarity glows in the cracks created by the curtains closed incorrectly. Emilio cannot decide whether to cross; he starts to walk, sticking to the wall, with the rain against him, protected by the overhanging edges of the buildings. Lucid, shivering from the cold, he imagines his father's body laid out among the flowers of an empty room with waxed floors; sitting on a chair, alone, the woman with the party dress cries under the sickly light. The wheels of the cars make a soft sound on the wet cement. Emilio stops under a store's awning. In the window there is a wire mannequin wearing a pink-colored silk slip. He lights a cigarette, covering the match with the hollow of his hand. He hears the murmur of the rain on the canvas and feels the warm smoke entering his lungs. An ample, geometric plaza opens up on the other side of the street. Near the corner there is a taxi stand. One of the cab drivers checks the air in his tires. Toward the back, the trees stir without sound. The lamps from the stoplight seem to burn in the haze. He waits for the light to change and starts to cross. He feels a slight pain in his neck and his eyes burn. He checks the time and gets in a taxi. "It's twelve twenty," he thinks. The driver drives with just one hand, his body angled against the window. The city grows quiet under the water, in the uncertain light of noon. *Dear son: it was difficult for us to talk, but I know that you have always loved me and you never judged me. I ask you not to judge me now, either. There is nothing to say about these things. It is simply about having a little courage, or not even that. I am very tired, so tired no one can imagine. I am a man who tried to live the life that seemed the most just to him. I have failed in many things but I do not regret anything. I have a few books that I'd like you to have. I'd also like you to wear my watch. There is not much more: it will serve to cover the costs that this may cause. I don't want a ceremony, I don't want flowers. I want my body to lie directly in the earth, like, as I believe, the Jews do. I feel calm, it is six in the afternoon. I hold you close to my heart. I would have liked to have seen you one more time. Your father.* As he finished reading he ripped the letter in uneven pieces, gently, letting the paper drift into the wet wind. He rode watching the streets open up like tunnels, until the taxi stopped in front of a building with glass walls. He looked at his face in the elevator mirror. He walked down the carpeted hallway. A window opened on the rear wall. Below, the city was a white surface. The sea could be seen in between the buildings. The woman took a while to open, but when she appeared she smiled at him, not surprised, disheveled and drowsy.

"Well, well," she said, and moved her soft body to let him enter. "What a surprise."

The apartment was nearly empty, lit by the greenish light of a bare bulb hanging from the ceiling. The woman closed the door and turned toward him, lifting her sweet, doll-like face.

"Did you come to bring me luck?"

"Yes," Emilio said, and hugged her. "Yes."

Muffled music came from a radio in between the blankets of the unmade bed.

"Do you like it?" she said. "It's Puccini's Tosca."

MOUSY BENITEZ SANG BOLEROS

1

I shall never know for sure whether the Viking was trying to tell me what really took place in the Club Atenas that dawn, or if he wanted to get rid of his guilt, or if he was crazy. The story, in any case, was confusing, disconnected: pieces of his life, the disheartened Scandinavian war cry, and a crumpled cutout from *El Gráfico* rolled up in rags, with the Viking's very fine and luminous face looking straight at the camera.

From the start I had suspected that something was not right in the story told by the newspapers. But if I had some hope that he himself would decipher the events, it was erased as soon as I saw him arrive, distrustful, his face pocked by the sun, hiding his hands in his chest, with an obsessive and brutal air. He moved slowly, in a gentle swaying, and it was fatal to remember, with melancholy, of his way of walking the ring so indolently to keep distance, of his natural elegance, coming out swinging and working his hips to prevent infighting. There he was, cornered, his back against the wall, half-lost; he looked toward the end of the hallway without seeing the afternoon's last light, already dissolving among the poplars and the bars of the hospice. I handed him a cigarette; he made a hollow with his hands to shelter the flame, without touching me, embarrassed by the grease spots that stained his skin; he smoked, dejected, until almost not being able to remove the embers from his lips; then he remained still, with his eyes empty, and all of a sudden he was poking around in the pockets of his shirt, digging out a bunch of rags which he started to open up neatly until he found the withered cutout from *El Gráfico*, where one could see his face, young and blurry, next to the face of Archie Moore. He stretched the paper out toward me, breathing with his mouth open, speaking with difficulty, with a guttural, incomprehensible voice, piling up words without any order until, by chance, he became silent; he looked at me, as if waiting for an answer, before beginning anew, returning every single time to that dawn in the Club Atenas in La Plata, to the destroyed, little body of Mousy Benítez flung on the floor, face up, as if he were floating in the quivering light of daybreak.

Somehow the entire story leads to the Club Atenas; the story, or what is worth telling of it, begins there the afternoon in which Mousy Benítez approached the Viking's desolate and fierce figure and in a show of loyalty, of unforeseen loyalty toward that outlandish monster, he, with his squalid little body and his face like a titi monkey's, went up to the others, to the ones who were harassing the Viking, and snatched the trophy — the only insignia or heraldic shield that the Viking had managed to conquer in years of lost battles and heroic failures — away from them. He shooed them away, furious, on the verge of tears; then he retreated next to the Viking and tried to calm him, not knowing that he sought out his own death.

No one will ever know what happened, but it is certain that one must look for the secret in that broken-down boxing club whose dilapidated walls and peaked roof rose up at the end of an empty street: there, one afternoon in May of '51, the man who years later would find himself obligated to be called The Viking, put a pair of gloves on for the first time, threw his left leg forward, raised his hands, put his guard up, and started boxing.

Introverted and delicate, he was agile, quick, and too elegant to be efficient. He moved with the looseness of a lightweight and everyone praised the purity of his style, but it was impossible to win with those punches that resembled caresses. Deep down, he had not been born to be a boxer, and even less a heavyweight, with his sweet face like a gallant from the silent movies, with his svelte and romantic figure he would have played a better role anywhere else; but he was a boxer without having chosen to be so, fatality of being born with that splendid body, and so close to the Club Atenas. It was sad to see him resist, intrepidly and without a shadow of a doubt, the assaults of the brutal mastodons of the category. He was rather a man to be boxing among lightweights, at the most in some welterweight; in any case, inexplicably and in a kind of betrayal that carried him toward disaster, his body, as strict as a cane, always surpassed the ninety-kilogram mark even if he starved himself. He never got anywhere and he never had another virtue other than the purity of his style, a crazy obstinacy to assimilate the punishment, a stubbornness, a pride that forced him to stay on his feet, absorbing the assault even if he was destroyed.

He reached the height of his career one anonymous afternoon: one afternoon in August of '53, in the half-lit gymnasium of Luna Park, when he stayed on his feet against Archie Moore in the only training session that the world champion held in Buenos Aires before fighting the Uruguayan Dogomar Martínez. It was a vertiginous afternoon that was always painful for him to remember afterward. No one dared to be Archie Moore's sparring partner; he decided to do it because he still had that inalterable quality, let us say adolescent, of disregarding the risks and of trusting without the least hesitation in the strength of his senseless will; full of hope, he thought this was his chance, he convinced himself that he was capable of fighting at the same level for five, three-minute rounds with that perfect boxing machine that was Archie Moore.

He was alone for a long time, sitting in a corner near the showers, waiting. He watched the oily light that fell from the bulbs in their wire caging, mixing with the clarity of the afternoon, without thinking anything, trying to forget that Moore was, at that time, one of the three or four greatest boxers in the history of boxing. At one point he thought he was falling asleep, cradled by the confusing sounds of the men who moved toward the back, but suddenly the photographers arrived like a whirlwind and he found himself in the ring with Archie Moore in front of him. They started lightly, exchanging leads and working the ropes. Moore was shorter, wore red gloves and little velvet boots. The Viking felt very stiff, tied up, too attentive to what was happening outside the ring, to the powder flashes that went off unexpectedly each time Moore moved. Besides, he felt curiosity rather than fear. Wanted to know how much the punches from a world champion were going to hurt. Shortly Moore had cornered him twice, but both times he managed to slip away by faking with his hips. The champion stood out of place, facing an empty space, and stopped smiling. The Viking started going around in circles, always out of reach; Moore jabbed with his left, stationary, swaying, and all of a sudden he would drive at him with fulminating speed. The Viking did nothing but look at Moore's hands, trying to anticipate, with the dark feeling that the other could guess what he was going to do. One of those times he moved a little slower and Moore hit him with two right crosses and a left to the body; it seemed to the Viking that something was breaking inside. Moore touched him softly with the left, as if taking distance, faked taking a step to the side looking to set up the right, and when the Viking moved to cover himself, Moore's left slashed down like a whip and found him midway. The Viking's eyes clouded over; he raised his face looking for air but saw only the gymnasium's globes of light, spinning. Moore leaned away, without touching him, waiting for him to collapse. The Viking felt himself become cross-legged, swayed to let himself go, but held himself up on something, on air, who knows on what he supported himself; the fact is that when he lowered his face, his hands where once again up on guard.

From then on Moore started to go after him seriously, to knock him out. When they where in the middle of the ring and there was room, the Viking got by with his leg work, but each time Moore cornered him against the ropes he felt like lifting his arms and starting to cry. Soon he was navigating in an opaque fog, without being able to understand how they could hit him so hard, all of his energy concentrated in not removing his feet from the earth: the only proof that he was still alive. He tried to stay loyal to his style and come out boxing, but Moore was too quick and always got there first. Toward the end he had lost everything, except for that fatal instinct that made him look for the most classic way out, to maintain a certain elegance in spite of being half-blind, undone by the crossing punches and the jab combinations and the uppercuts which stopped him as if he were continuously running into a wall. At that point Moore himself looked like a merciful man, forced to hit because that was his job, with a gentle lightning bolt of respect and consideration illuminating his slightly-crossed eyes, a kind of supplication, as if he were telling him to let himself fall so that he would not have to keep hitting him.

When it all ended he almost did not realize it. He continued to cover himself and he did not even lower his arms when he saw the photographers come up, as if he were afraid that they thought Moore had been able to knock him out in the end. Only when someone put him next to Moore and he saw a photographer in front of him, did he understand that he had managed to resist; then he looked at the camera, became rigid and tried to concentrate so that he would not close his eyes when the flash went off. He got down from the ring thinking about each move, stunned by the pain but triumphant and satisfied, having acquired forever a confidence in his courage and his manhood, as if he had really fought Moore for the world title, between tides of intoxicating fame and without seeing the emptiness, the sickly clarity dissolving the faces, the silhouettes of the men surrounding Moore, without anyone to look after him, alone as he would never be again.

2

In the five years that followed there was nothing other than a long succession of heroic massacres, in which he could only offer the strange beauty of his face—which often filled the ringside ladies with uneasiness—and a grim haughtiness, a perfectionist's mania that was imperceptible to anyone not with him between the ropes. Of course the feelings of the ringside ladies were always a secret anxiety; none of his rivals ever turned out to be gentleman enough to respect that suicidal pride.

So his career broke off, without any surprises, one night in February of '56, in the Club Atenas. In that nearly-deserted shed he boxed for the last time, facing a brutal unknown with a turbid look who went after him for ten rounds throwing heavy blows, which he opposed only with that absurd perseverance and the futile purity of his style, the elegant work with the hips that seemed destined to find all the punches that were floating in the air. He fell four times but finished standing, cloudy and staggering, his gaze fixed into space. When the bell rang they dragged him to his corner; he looked at them, surly, his eyes very open, as if he were hallucinating or dazed, his face broken, blurred by the blood.

He never decided to stop boxing, because to do so he would

have had to doubt himself and it was useless to assume that he would do this; they simply stopped offering him fights, they watched him circling around the offices of the promoters, they saw him arrive at the gymnasium every morning with his handbag and start to train, reticent, inexhaustible, inspiring that irritated pity that tends to be caused by an overvaluation and an excess in confidence. Self-assured and ruined, he never asked for anything other than a chance to fight again to show what he was worth. Finally, when he was about to starve to death, someone shook him out of his lethargy and hooked him up as a professional fighter with a wrestling troupe. There, at least, his grayish eyes, his delicate, aristocratic face were worth something; he would get into the ring with a red beard that embarrassed him, and with a kind of horned helmet to justify his fighting name. He had to spread his arms wide and invent a spectacular rite that, according to the promoter, was the Viking greeting. He did it poorly, awkwardly, and without realizing it he tried always to face away from the audience, as if he did not want them to recognize him.

The troupe toured through the interior; he would spend the afternoons locked inside the broken down rooms of the sad, little, provincial hotels, flung face up on the bed, waiting for the night, waiting for the absurd jumps and the laughter, without anything to console him other than digging out, every once in a while, the yellowish cutout from *El Gráfico* in which he appeared, his triumphant and young face next to Archie Moore's. He would spend hours smoothing the paper out against the table, trying to undo the wrinkles that were deforming his face in the picture, slicing his beautiful, blond face that seemed to have aged, cracked on the brittle paper.

Everyone put up with him because he was useful to them, because his melancholic expression and his very tall figure, the reddish mane and the beard in the wind, attracted the audience who did not seem to notice his awkwardness, his absent air that showed openly that he was thousands of kilometers from that roped-off square elevated in the middle of a plaza.

To excuse his indifference they ended up saying that he was Swedish or Norwegian, that he did not speak one word of Spanish; and that fable invented to strengthen the myth favored his surliness, his silence. With time, everyone ended up believing it, even the person who had made it up, and perhaps he himself became convinced that he had been born in some remote country, of which he only still had left a vague nostalgia.

He was in this for more than two years during which he barely spoke with the others, was always distant and alone, trapped by the vertiginous and monotonous succession of little towns, of brutal faces and Viking greetings. No one was surprised when he disappeared unexpectedly one afternoon. The troupe had landed in La Plata and he left without telling anyone, suddenly, as if he were obeying a calling, without taking anything other than an old cardboard suitcase, the pseudonym which he was to keep until his death, and the beard brightening his face. He walked through the deserted streets in the burning heat of siesta-time in February, covered up in a black tricot turtleneck, attracting attention with such a tall body, with his outlandish figure, without looking at the people who turned around to watch that blond giant pass by; he traversed the thick, sweet aroma of the basswood and sought out the Club Atenas like someone returning home after a storm. He had nothing to offer other than the same obstinacy, but he stayed until he brought about the tragedy.

It was there, after crossing the Atenas' dilapidated lobby and ducking down through the small door that led to the gymnasium, that he saw for the first time the diminutive body of Mousy Benítez. The kid, a seventeen-year-old featherweight with a lot of promise, but who could not decide between his innate talent for boxing and his desire to be a singer of boleros, was toward the rear, lost between the ropes and the smell of resin. And it is said that he barely made a gesture, a slight swaying, and that this was his way of saying that he had always been waiting for him. The two looked at each other, nearly motionless, and after an instant Mousy kept hitting the punching bag, which was taller than him, with his small, delicate hands, his whole face concentrated in an effort to look fierce. The Viking continued to walk toward the middle, as if he were looking for him, while Mousy hugged the punching bag and saw him approach, already fascinated by that figure, framed in a phantasmal air by the siesta sun coming in through the clouded windows. He stood watching him, a slight smile soothed upon his womanly little mouth, as if he caught a glimpse of the Viking's haughtiness and secret rage, or better yet, as if he could guess that that haughtiness and that rage were dedicated to him.

Perhaps due to this, from then on Mousy was the only one who seemed to pay attention to the Viking's existence. Captivated, attentive to his slightest gestures, he watched over him, imitating strange signs, facial expressions, murmurings, well-balanced representations in which his body acquired the harmony and splendor of a small statue. These celebrations culminated when the Viking was nearby: then Mousy would drop what he was doing, bend his neck back, fix his eyes on the Viking's desolate face, and with his high-pitched voice, very sad and almost like a woman's, he would sing a bolero from the golden era, in the style of Julio Jaramillo.

The Viking did not seem to hear him or know that he existed, as if he moved in another dimension, always absent. He would withdraw into a corner with his eyes lost and spend hours, dazed by the rustling of the gymnasium, without doing anything other than shifting his position every once in a while. Sometimes, however, he seemed excited, he would move about nervously with a blue glow in his eyes and suddenly, in the most unexpected moments, he would be struck by a strange restlessness, he would tremble lightly, he would start to murmur in a very low voice, agitated and groping at the air, until he ended up enraged, telling in an indecipherable tone a confusing story: the story of his boxing session with Archie Moore. He would repeat the moves, boxing alone, crouched and with his guard up, throwing timid, sluggish blows. He would jump or move, heavy, awkward, trying to rescue something of all of that, even a fleeting vision of that pact with Moore, of that mad, senseless, and never-valued heroism. The others (all those who used the Atenas as a temple of their dreams, of their catastrophes) would form a circle around him, they would rile him up by cheering him on, laughing and knowing that at the end, unfailingly, sweating and tired, breathing with his mouth open, he would dig through his shirt with sluggish and careful manners until he found the cutout from *El Gráfico*, which he would hold up firmly but distant from his body, in a gesture of sadness, of dejection, and secret pride.

Mousy was the only one who seemed impressed, the only one who looked at the picture from the cutout, at the Viking's face, a little battered, that could be deciphered in the piece of paper. The others made jokes, laughed, while Mousy moved away, seemed to hide, taking refuge in a corner; from there he would watch over everyone who crowded around the Viking's swaying body. Afraid, without finding the courage to intervene, he watched with pain as the Viking tried to tell about that fight in any way possible, about Moore's fulminating speed and his little velvet boots.

And that afternoon, when someone grabbed the piece of paper, the Viking remained motionless, as if he did not understand; then it seemed like something clouded his eyes, because he passed his hand across his face and suddenly he was in the middle of them, without seeing Mousy next to him, enraged and diminutive, insulting them and making them retreat, until he finally turned around toward the Viking and touched him lightly with the palms of his hands, slowly, herding him as if he were a large, sick animal. He took him aside, far from the others, and began talking to him in a low voice, lulling him, while the Viking stopped moving and moaning, already calmed, his eyes lost in space, his beautiful face peaceful.

From that day on they were always together, separate from the rest. They would withdraw to a corner toward the back of the gymnasium, still, silent, and all of a sudden Mousy would start to sing boleros, very quietly, just for the Viking, letting himself go with the high notes as if he were going to fall apart.

It is said that in those times the Viking seemed to have been reborn. He started to enter the ring with Mousy and act as his sparring partner. Some attribute the cause of everything to this, they speak of an accident, of an out-of-control hand. In any case, it was comical to see them exchange punches: Mousy minute, nearly a child, jumping nimbly, with his face like a titi monkey's, next to the large, curved mass of the Viking, moving heavily. Just one of the Viking's punches would have sufficed to break Mousy in two; Mousy, however, entered the ring self-assured and strutting about, like a trainer in a bear cage. They would put their guard up and begin a simulacrum of a fight, the Viking standing pat in the middle, Mousy dancing constantly around him. The Viking would punch him delicately, as if he were petting him, and put his face out with impunity, proud of having recovered his fabulous resistance to punishment. Finally Mousy would get tired of hitting and would dedicate himself to jumping rope. The Viking would sit to a side, his eyes fixed on the other's face, tense with the effort, his whole body shining with sweat.

When afternoon fell, the two would get into the showers together. Mousy's shrieks could be heard from outside; spending hours under the water, he would sing with his eyes closed while the Viking got dressed and waited for him, stretched out on one of the wooden benches without a back, his hands behind his head, dozing off until Mousy appeared, his skin bluish, smelling like coconut soap; and then Mousy would start getting dressed, elegant and theatrical, making facial expressions in front of the fogged mirror. The two would go out to walk through the city in the late afternoon, and people would stop to watch them as if they had come from another world, Mousy looking like a jockey but dressed like a dandy, walking next to that melancholic giant with the reddish mane.

They always ended up around the train station sitting at a table, on the sidewalk of the bar *Rayo*, under the trees, drinking dark beer and breathing the soft air of summer. They spent hours there as night fell, watching the movement of the station, guessing at the arrival of the trains by the torrent of people who passed in front of them. They did not speak, they did not do anything other than watch the street and drink beer, peaceful, as if they were not there; until finally, without either one of them saying anything, they would get up and leave, led by Mousy who looked attentively to one side and the other before crossing the street, always walking a little behind the Viking, as if he were herding him through the cars.

That is how they spent what was left of the summer: more and more isolated, perfecting between the two of them the final secret of the story. Everyone thought that during that time Mousy spent the nights in the Atenas. They were even seen, one morning, sleeping together, Mousy's head resting on the Viking's chest; it looked like he was cradling a doll. In any case, no one predicted or could have known what was to happen that night; the light from the Club was seen until dawn and someone heard Mousy's high-pitched, smooth, and out-of-tune voice singing "El relicario." A dense wind blew all night, dragging the smell of burnt wood from the river. It seemed strange that no one came out to open up; the door was broken, as if the wind had taken it apart, and on the other side, in the quivering light of dawn filtering in through the windows, they found Mousy, dying, shattered by blows, and the Viking on the floor, crying and petting the head, which was dirty with blood and dust. The whole gymnasium empty, the soft murmuring of the wind between the sheet metal, and toward the back the curved figure of the Viking hugging Mousy's body, whose face was destroyed and whose womanly little mouth had a smile upon it, like a dark sign of love, of indolence, or of gratitude.

THE GLASS BOX

for Juan José Saer

After the accident, Rinaldi and I are always together. Right now, for example, he is sitting there, sunk into the small, low chair, breathing with difficulty. He does not speak but he studies my reactions. A bit flushed, he aims his bird's profile at me. He smells of tobacco and stagnant water. I am convinced that he has seen everything. The news was in the papers—they do not say anything about me, barely an imprecise reference. It was an accident. Things would have taken place just the same had I not been there. The boy played in the plaza and the jungle gym blazed in the sun. I remember the events as if in a dream. A moment of weakness and a man's life loses all sense. The afternoon is clear and mild. The smell of the carnations from the flowerpots makes one think of death. We look at each other in silence. No remorse, only a vague fear, impersonal, almost anonymous. I speak in the present, it is so easy to speak in the present when already nothing can be changed. "Last night," Rinaldi says all of a sudden, "I thought you were complaining in your dreams." I smile at him, my face sweeter than his. A docile music is coming from the terrace; it mingles and is lost in the murmur of the city. In the room it is too hot. The air is balmy here. What did Rinaldi really see? That I do not know. *In the plaza the genteel Genz, stretched out on the wooden bench, adopts a distant tone. I know his ways and I am not surprised by that cunning expression, like someone who has set a trap. When I realize what he is going to do it is already too late. The darkness is in our hearts.* I quote from memory: there is nothing else. I can rest assured. I can rest assured? I fool myself deliberately. Why is he bent, if not, on recording the events? He keeps the journal in an unlocked box. He jots down thoughts, unsettling situations, opinions on my personality. *Today we went for a walk. He with an air of importance, I easygoing and smooth. We went to the dance hall which is on Rodríguez Peña and Sarmiento. Waxed floors, mirrors that multiply on the walls. Women that smell of cheap perfume, of honeysuckle. You buy tickets. Each dance costs 1,000 pesos. Genz chooses melodic songs to show off. Air of a dreamer. Dances all night with an arrogant woman, with blackish hair.*

Rinaldi is of Uruguayan nationality. He always speaks about Tacuarembó. His father was a professional cyclist. Champion of the Banda Oriental. One afternoon he showed me the yellow tricot jersey: Club Wanderers. We have lived together for one year but I know little about him. He came from nothing, from the benign semi-darkness of a bar where he drank, one after another, deep mugs of dark beer, dissolved in the calming fluttering of the fan's wooden blades. Striped shirt, silk suspenders, and a soft shine in his little cat-eyes. He speaks with an asthmatic gasping. "Wouldn't you (gasp) like to have (gasp) a beer (gasp)?" (He has also written about my manner of speaking. *At the Club América where I go often to play chess, I always find a very skinny man who is unhealthily shy and who speaks so quietly that no one knows what he is saying. To be polite you answer randomly, and the dialogue continues. Finally, yesterday—I had had a number of drinks—I told him: "You know Genz, you have never spoken with anyone in your life. Everyone lies to you." He was startled and responded with some murmur which I was unable to make out.*) I was alone at that time, lost in the city. An invisible man who goes through the world unnoticed. I wanted to start again. I wanted to start to live. Rinaldi took care of me. He looked kindly upon me, a smile sweetening his chapped face, and I felt happy. That is why I brought him to the boarding house, that is why I decided to share my room with him. Must it be said that I am a sentimentalist? Rather a weak man who never knew how to take care of himself. I do not know anything about Rinaldi. Now I realize it, now that I need to know something about his life. It is difficult to get him to speak about himself. *I am not used to talking about what is happening with me*—he has written in his diary. *It must be out of pride and also due to my awkwardness. I don't want secrets or moods of the soul; I am not a virgin to pretend to have an inner life.*

At the very beginning, however, he showed me a picture of a woman with a serious face who killed herself, according to him, out of love for him. We had gone out to dinner together and suddenly he started speaking about her. A confusing story, disjointed. I thought he was boasting. Who doesn't like to believe that they have caused a woman to die because of love for them? Later (three months ago, when I started reading his diary) I found a letter among his papers. *We never came together like we should have come together, crystal dreamer. Thus determined and to such terms subjected, my friend, can I content myself with such a life? It is not that unjust then for me to abandon the early mornings and late afternoons (which I have not bothered to look at for some time now, by the way), and the songs of the birds (I never liked birds), or the intimate satisfaction of seeing my daughters getting dressed to go dancing (they will do it just the same without me; even if I live, they will always be in need of something, or they will take shelter in the memory of a nanny whom they loved—they will say, they shall say—more than their own mother). You always knew how to explain things to me, and the explanations you gave me were true; for my part, I prefer to imagine, instead of knowing, the reasons why I won't survive this event; I am not 18 years old, nor 25, nor even 33. All the things my body has put up with: the drinking, the treatments to stop drinking. How much more can it take? You must understand, even now. But if I was to survive (or if I were to survive), I would imagine your smile. I will try to avoid any incursion into (any refuge behind) irony. Always. Your Dalia.* A woman with a flower's name. Sometimes I think that that story can be of use to me. A suicide always encapsulates the story of a crime. Perhaps I should escape, travel to Uruguay, find out the details. We are all guilty of something. Not just me. To know his secrets, like he knows mine. I was going to leave him the room. I told him, I chose the moment. Now it is too late, I am in his hands. A ridiculous expression. To leave. Search for another shelter in the city in which to put my body. Go back to being alone. No one to keep an eye on me and to wake up at night to listen to my dreams. I have been thinking for weeks. I am a cowardly man. I lack the courage necessary to choose between two alternatives. That is why everything happened. The accident, I mean. I remember it (I have already said this) as if it were a dream. The plaza, the pebbled flower beds, the glass box, the sound of Rinaldi's shoes on the pebbled flower beds. I remember, yes, the sour heat, the city's burning fumes. Rinaldi walked around in the room, half-naked. He paced from one spot to another, like a bug, fattened by beer and boredom; from one spot to another, until he stopped against the gloomy clarity of the window and told me that he needed money. An unexpected contingency had forced him to pawn his summer suit. He begged me to lend him some money to recover the suit because he had to meet a woman. He spoke of her with sarcasm, falsely. A young woman, seventeen years old, blond with blue eyes, who played the piano. Stretched out on the bed, I watched his face, clouded by the clarity of the morning. "The girl," he was saying, "her name is Nuty. She waits for me in a house with a garden, I sit among the flowers, underneath the arbor, and she plays piano for me. She plays Chopin, she plays Mozart, Beethoven." He walked around the room, sweaty and troubled, and I let him talk. Finally I told him that I'd give him money. "I will give you the money," I told him, "but I also want to let you know that I am leaving. I am leaving you the room." Rinaldi brushed his chest with the palm of his hand, attentive, skeptical. "Letting me know?" he said and began to smile. "You are going to leave the room to me?" There was something like a malicious throbbing in his little cat-eyes, a senseless brightness in the middle of his face. "Fine," he said, "fine." He opened the closet, looked for his only suit, a tartan flannel suit, and began to get dressed. "I have other plans," I told him. "Do you understand?" "Of course, yes, other plans," he said next to the half-opened door. "Of course," he said, and stepped into the raw light of the hallway. I was left alone. A room in a boarding house is like any other room in a boarding house: two beds, a closet, tall ceilings. The following day I was going to buy the newspaper to look for another place. I got up and looked out the window. In the patio a boy was playing, bouncing a rubber ball. I was thinking of everything I had to do before leaving. I was going to have to walk around the city, cross tiled lobbies, dark stairwells. Speak with fat, greasy women who would listen distrustfully to me. The details are always the worst. It is difficult to begin. I did not feel like doing anything. I remember that I sat on the bed and opened the box where Rinaldi hides his papers. *They have hired a very ugly woman in the boarding house. She takes care of the cleaning. She must be around fifty and her hair is gray. In two months I have been raped several times in a curious way by the old cleaning woman. Once in a while we argue like husband and wife.* His split handwriting. A man who writes. Who cares about Rinaldi's adventures? The cyclist's son sweating in his flannel suit. I should have followed him. Walked after him to see him faint and dissolve in the heat. I looked at my watch: it was twelve. Twelve. It is always too early or too late for what one wants to do. I started to move around the room in the pale light. I turned on the desk lamp. The sounds of a conversation came in through the window. "Do you believe I care what he might think? Drop dead, she said to him. I'm tired of everything," a woman's sharp, sad voice was saying. "As far as I'm concerned, honey, you know, in any case, I told him, what do I care? I'm free like a swallow." I could also write. Record events. I do not have the will to do it. Why do one thing instead of another? Immediately there was a knock on the door. It was the cleaning woman. Her name is Aurora. Every morning she comes to do the cleaning. She was singing as she worked. She was blond and her blue eyes sang, reflecting the glories of the day. She leant over so I would see her thighs. I find it a little unpleasant. She smells like a recently bathed baby. A smell too sweet, like loose flesh, like dead flowers. "Don't you know," she said, "that it's forbidden to use the electricity when it's light out?" She had turned around and was looking at me with an expression that did not correspond to her tone of voice. It was a dreamy, romantic expression. Desire continues to beat within her and makes her act like a young woman. I had to make love to her but it was out of common courtesy. She believes she is good at it. She squeezed my head against her chest in a fit of passion. For my part, I stirred distractedly in her sex. I was thinking about Rinaldi, crossing the city, suffocating in his flannel suit. *Aurora makes love like spiders do. She's avid and quick and only thinks of her own pleasure. She pushes, she presses my face against her arms, and immediately starts to moan, her eyes roll back into her head, her face dissolved in pleasure. I can't look at her body: it's soft, bloated, as if it were stuffed with cotton. In any case I prefer her to any other woman because she knows what she wants.* I felt empty and satisfied. Having forgotten me, Aurora sang and finished getting dressed. She was carried off by a payador from Lavalle's time, she sang, when the year of '40 was dying. He was going to live alone, without imagining friendships that don't exist. Alone like a bird. He was still young to begin again. Aurora had started to clean the room once again. She would lift a chair and put it back in the same place. "You can't stay here," she said. "Go, go. Let a person get their work done." She spoke without looking at me, staring down at the floor. I went out to the hallway, into the hallway's blinding glare. I like the light of summer, violent and raw; it seems to be made of glass. As I crossed the patio I heard the cleaning woman singing. Her voice escorted me, and for a moment I was able to think that it was a farewell. (Now that everything has already happened, I know that it was a farewell.) The city seemed dead and I felt happy. I let myself walk out of habit toward the plaza. It was a quiet plaza, similar to any plaza in Buenos Aires, with plants and flowers and mothers who walk their children and their dogs. I looked for a bench among the coolness of the trees. Everything was still, beautifully calm. Who could have foreseen what was to happen? A jungle gym with sheet metal panels, tall and fragile. The boy had red hair and wore a blue shirt. "See," he said to me. "It's golf." He extended a glass box to me, a game: you had to make a steel sphere go into one of the holes, painted sky-blue. I entertained myself watching the little silver ball moving and jumping around. "Are you staying?" the boy asked me. "I'm going to play. Won't you watch the golf game?" He moved away a little and smiled at me. He must have been ten years old. The light was burning up the asphalt, but the boy's face was strangely attenuated and sweetened by the shade of the trees. I held the box in my fingers. The metal sphere rolled around the holes and got away toward the sides. Laying back on the bench I watched the boy who had begun to climb the jungle gym, holding on to the wooden crossbars with his hands and feet. A warm air was blowing and the streets were deserted. I was struck by a strange happiness. I had proven to Rinaldi that I was capable of deciding for myself. "I don't care about anything," I thought. "When I decide to, I can do whatever I want." The certainty that sooner or later I would have to return to the room and confront Rinaldi, however, attenuated my happiness like a dark premonition. Perhaps he has always lied to me, perhaps at that moment he was already watching me. *In the plaza the genteel Genz, stretched out on the wooden bench, adopts a distant tone. I know his ways and I am not surprised by that cunning expression, like someone who has set a trap. When I realize what he is going to do it is already too late. The darkness is in our hearts.* A yellow truck stopped at the corner. A delivery truck, the back covered with canvas. The driver, from a distance, looked like a puppet; he got out with a brown paper-wrapped package and crossed toward a house with a stone entrance. Everything became still again. I would have liked for that stillness never to end. Just being there on the bench, with the glass box in my hand, playing, trying to make a metal sphere go into a sky-blue hole. I did not wish for anything other than to stay there, in the cool shade, waiting for the arrival of night. The wind made the sheet metal panels vibrate with a gentle sound. With effort, I looked up. The sky was a stain between the leaves of the trees. The boy was at the top of the jungle gym. It was beautiful to see him there, so high up, dissolved in the radiance. He was still, with his body arched, looking at the city; then he began to descend, slowly, his body facing the metal panelings. He stopped and moved a foot in mid-air, searching for a place to steady himself with the tip of his shoe. He, too, looked like a puppet. A wax puppet. I had that thought and was late in realizing that the bar he was going to step on was loose. "He looks like a wax puppet," I thought, and watched him move a foot in mid-air without seeing the broken cross-bar. It was hard for me to think; everything was slow and heavy. The jungle gym faded, far from me, as if it were behind glass. The boy had pressed himself against the sheet metal panels; he did not dare look down. He was pale, frail and pale, his red hair on his forehead. He glanced down just a little and we looked at each other for a moment. "He can't decide," I thought. "He sees me sitting among the trees. He can't decide." He wavered, hesitant, as if frightened, his body stiff. He took a long time before moving; at that moment, the truck started up. It pulled off from the other side of the street. It was an instant. As if something had broken. First I heard the noise and then the boy's body hit the cement. I felt the coolness of the glass box against the palm of my hand. "It's golf," I thought sluggishly. Then I saw Rinaldi, crossing the plaza before me. His approach lasted forever, as if he were walking in a dream. Now I think of the sound of the gravel underneath the soles of his shoes. I could hear the crunching of the gravel underneath the soles of his shoes. I thought: "I was going to warn him." I thought: "He looked like a wax puppet." Rinaldi took care of everything. I followed him, half-asleep. When I discovered that I was carrying the glass box with me I dropped it between the flowers. It must still be there, among the honeysuckles. Perhaps I should go look for it. It is incredible, but several times I was about to tell Rinaldi that I had dropped the box. "It's a game," the boy said, "golf." When I think about the boy I always see him in the same position: suspended in the air, his arms crossed, engulfed in the fog that the sheet metal panels seemed to give off, suspended and almost floating, unable to move. This I should discuss with Rinaldi. He is sitting before me (I believe I have said this) in a small, low chair. I look at him and it is just like looking at myself in a mirror. *Genz and I always under the covers of sin. Shoulder to shoulder, the frail Siamese carefully consults a strategy manual. Brave hearts, pure soul. Who am I to hide? Sudden peacefulness under the lights of the dying summer.* I get up in the middle of the night, naked, and silently rummage through his papers: I expect him to write the truth, but find phrases, soft lies. No one is capable of writing the truth. Aurora has watered the garden; the smell of wet earth cools the air. "Let's go," Rinaldi says to me now. "I want to go out for a walk." I follow him, I go after him. I do not have the willpower to say no. The street descends between decayed walls and gardens behind iron gates. We walk. There is no need to talk. We look at each other in silence. Nothing like a secret to unite men. If this understanding is what the world calls friendship, then the relationship between Rinaldi and I is, undoubtedly, one of friendship. I understand that his feelings for me have no objective other than to use me in whatever way most pleases him. This idea, logically, does not make me very happy; in any case, I cannot expect that his opinion of me be different. Who could have foreseen this fate for me in my distant youth?

THE MADWOMAN AND THE STORY OF THE CRIME

1

Fat, diffused, melancholy, the fil-à-fil Nile-green suit floating on his body, Almada went out with an air of secret euphoria to try to erase his dejection. The streets were already growing quiet; dark and lustrous, their mild downward slope made him advance placidly, holding the brim of his hat when the wind from the river touched his face. At that moment the coperas were starting their first shifts. At any given time there are men looking for women, they walk through the city under the pale sun, cross furtively toward the nightclubs that in the afternoons let a sweet music fall upon the city. Almada felt lost, full of fear and contempt. The memory of Larry returned with his discouragement: the woman's distant body, soft on the leather stool, knees apart, the red hair against the *New Deal's* sky-blue lamps. To see her from afar, in plain daylight, the worn out skin, the shadows under her eyes, swaying against the meek mauve light that came down from the sky: haughty, drunk, indifferent, as if he were just a plant or a bug. "To be able to humiliate her once," he thought. "Break her in two to make her groan and give in."

At the corner, the sight of the *New Deal* was an ochre stain, corroded, even more perverted under the six P.M. haze. Standing in front of it, stocky, conceited, Almada lit a cigarette and lifted his face as if searching the air for Larry's malignant perfume. He felt strong now, capable of anything, capable of going into the cabaret and pulling her out by the arm and slapping her around until she obeyed him. "Years that I've wanted to take off," he thought suddenly. "Set up on my own in Panama, Quito, Ecuador." To one side, lying down in a doorway, he saw the dirty bundle of a woman who slept wrapped in rags. Almada pushed her with his foot.

"Hey, you," he said.

The woman sat up, groping at the air, and raised her face as if blinded. "What's your name?" he asked.

"Who?"

"You. Or can't you hear me?"

"Echevarne Angélica Inés," she said, rigid. "Echevarne Angélica Inés, they call me Anahí."

"And what are you doing here?"

"Nothing," she said. "Will you give me money?"

"Aha, you want money?"

The woman hugged a man's old overcoat that was wrapped around her body like a tunic.

"Okay," he said. "If you kneel down and kiss my feet I'll give you 1,000 pesos."

"Huh?"

"See? Look," Almada said waving the bill in his little stubby fingers. "Kneel down and I'll give it to you."

"I am her, I am Anahí. I'm the sinner, the gypsy."

"Did you hear me?" Almada said. "Or are you drunk?"

"The Macarena, oh Macarena, all in tulles," the woman sang and began to kneel down on top of the rags that covered her skin until she sank her face between Almada's legs. He looked at her from above, majestic, a moist shine in his little cat-eyes.

"Here you go. I'm Almada," he said, and handed her the bill. "Buy yourself some perfume."

"The sinner. Queen and mother," she said. "There was never in this whole country a man more beautiful than Juan Bautista Bairoletto, the jockey."

The sounds of a piano could be heard weakly through the nightclub's high window, indecisive. Almada closed his hands in his pockets and headed toward the music, toward the blood-colored curtains of the entrance.

"The Macarena, oh Macarena," the madwoman was singing. "All in tulles and silks, the Macarena, oh, all in tulles," sang the madwoman.

Antúnez entered the yellowish hallway of the boarding house at Viamonte and Reconquista, peaceful, already meek, thankful for that subtle combination of life's events that he called his destiny. He had been living with Larry for one week. They used to meet every time that he would linger at the *New Deal* without choosing or wanting to admit that he went because of her; later, in bed, the two used each other with coldness and efficacy, slowly, perversely. Antúnez would wake up past noon and go down to the street, having already forgotten the light's sour glare on the half-closed shutters. Until at last one morning, without any warning, she stood naked in the middle of the room, and as if she were speaking to herself asked him not to leave. Antúnez broke out laughing: "What for?" he asked. "Stay?" he said, a heavy, aging man. "What for?" he had said, but it was already decided, because at that moment he had begun to be aware of his inexorable decadence, of the signs of that failure which he had chosen to call his destiny. So he let himself stay in that room, without anything to do except lean out the little iron balcony to watch the downward slope of Viamonte and see its approach, sluggish, engulfed in the haze of sunrise. He became accustomed to the way she had of coming in, bringing with her the fatigue of the men that had bought her drinks, and going over as if blinded to leave the money on the night table. He also became accustomed to the pact, to the secret and dear decision not to speak about the money, as if they both knew that she paid in that manner for the way he had of protecting her from the fears that would suddenly come upon her of dying or of going crazy.

"There's little play left for her and me," he thought, reaching the turn in the hallway; at that moment, before opening the door to the room, he knew that the woman had left him, and that everything was beginning to fall apart. What he could not have imagined was that on the other side he would find misfortune and pity, the signs of death in the open drawers and the empty closet, in Larry's jars, perfumes, and powders thrown all over the floor: the farewell or the good-bye written with lipstick on the dresser's mirror, like a notice that the woman had wanted to leave for him before leaving.

He came Almada came he came to take me he knows everything about us he came to the cabaret and he's like a pest a piece of trash oh my god leave please I beg you save yourself Juan he came to get me this afternoon he's a rat forget me I beg you forget me as if I Larry had never been in your life however much you want to don't look for me because he is going to kill you

Antúnez read the shaky letters, drawn like a net over his reflected face on the surface of the mirror.

2

Emilio Renzi was interested in linguistics but he earned his living doing reviews for the newspaper *El Mundo*. Having spent five years in the University specializing on the phonology of Trubetzkoi and ending up doing half-page write-ups on the desolate national literary panorama was without a doubt the cause of his melancholy; of that appearance, concentrated and somewhat metaphysical, that made him look like a character from a Roberto Arlt novel.

The guy who did police stories was sick the afternoon when the news of Larry's murder reached the newspaper. Old-man Luna decided to send Renzi to cover the account because he thought that forcing him to get involved in that story of cheap whores and small-time pimps would be good for him. They had found the woman stabbed repeatedly around the corner from the *New Deal*; the only witness to the crime was a half-crazed beggar who said her name was Angélica Echevarne. When they found her she was cradling the corpse as if it were a doll and repeating an incomprehensible story. That same morning the police detained Juan Antúnez, the guy who lived with the copera, and the affair appeared to be resolved.

"Try to see if you can invent something that we can use," old-man Luna told him. "Go to the police station; at six they let the press in."

At the police station, Renzi found just one journalist, a certain Rinaldi, who covered crime for the newspaper *La Prensa*. The guy was tall and his skin looked like he had just come out of the water. They were led into a small room painted sky-blue that resembled a movie theater: four lamps illuminated a kind of wooden stage with a violent light. Through there they brought out a haughty man who covered his face with his handcuffed hands; immediately the place filled with photographers who took snapshots from every angle. The guy seemed to be floating in a fog, and when he lowered his hands he looked at Renzi with soft eyes.

"It was not me," he said. "It was Almada, the fat guy, but he's protected from higher up."

Uncomfortable, Renzi felt that the man was speaking only to him, and was urging him to help.

"I'm sure he did it," Rinaldi said when they took him away. "I can smell a criminal a hundred meters away: they all have the same expression of a cat that pissed on itself, they all say that it wasn't them and speak as if they were dreaming."

"I thought he was telling the truth."

"They always seem to tell the truth. There's the madwoman."

The old woman came in looking at the light and moved on the platform with a slight swaying, as if she were bound. As soon as he heard her, Renzi turned on his tape recorder.

"I have seen everything I have seen as if I saw all the insides of my body the ganglions the entrails the heart that belongs that belonged and will belong to Juan Bautista Bairoletto the jockey for that man I am telling you leave here enemy evil-spirit or can't you see that he wants to tear my skin off and make sheen lace tulle clothing braiding the gypsy Anahí's hair the Macarena oh Macarena you're a wretched woman you have no soul and the shine in that hand a flint I'll drink acid I swear if you come near me I'll drink acid sinner woman mad with envy because I'm clean of all evil I am a saint Echevarne Angélica Inés they call me Anahí Hitler was right when he said all Entrerrianos must be killed I am a witch and I am a gypsy and I am the queen that sews a tulle that hand's shine must be covered a flint the shine that made her die why do you take off the mask little masquerader who saw me or didn't see me and spoke to her of that money Mother Mary Mother Mary in the doorway Anahí was a gypsy and was queen and was friends with Evita Perón and where is purgatory if it wasn't in Lanús where they took the veiled Virgin in that machine with a tulle bun to cover her face that was white from innocence."

"It sounds like a parody of Macbeth," Rinaldi, erudite, whispered. "You remember, don't you? The story told by a madman that doesn't mean anything."

"By an idiot, not by a madman," Renzi corrected him. "By an idiot. And who told you that it doesn't mean anything?"

The woman kept talking, her face to the light.

"Why do they call me a traitor do you know why I will tell you because I was loved by the most beautiful man on this land Juan Bautista Bairoletto jockey with a poncho swollen with air it's a balloon a fat balloon that floats under the yellow light don't get close to me if you get close to me I'm telling you don't touch me with the sword because in the light is where I have seen everything I have seen as if I saw all the insides of my body the ganglions the entrails the heart that belongs that belonged and will belong."

"She's starting again," Rinaldi said.

"Maybe she's trying to make herself understood."

"Who? Her? But can't you see how nuts she is?" he said as he got up from the box seat. "Are you coming?"

"No. I'm staying."

"Listen old man. Don't you realize she always repeats the same thing since they found her?"

"That's why," Renzi said, adjusting the tape in the recorder. "That's why I want to listen: because she always repeats the same thing."

Three hours later Emilio Renzi was unfurling upon the surprised desk of old-man Luna a literal transcription of the madwoman's monologue, underlined with different colored pencils and covered with marks and numbers.

"I have proof that Antúnez did not kill the woman. Another did it, a guy he named, a certain Almada. Almada, the fat guy."

"What do you know?" Luna said, sarcastically. "So Antúnez says it was Almada and you believe him."

"No. It's the madwoman who says it, the madwoman who's been repeating the same thing for ten hours without saying anything. But precisely because she repeats the same thing she can be understood. There is a series of rules in linguistics, a code that is used to analyze psychotic language."

"Tell me kid," Luna said slowly. "Are you putting me on?"

"Hold on. Let me talk for a minute. In a delirium someone who is mad repeats, or better still, is forced to repeat certain verbal structures that are fixed, like a mold, you see, a mold which he fills with words. To analyze this structure there are thirty-six verbal categories called logical operators. They're like a map, you put them on top of what the person says and you realize that the delirium is ordered, that these formulas are being repeated. What does not fit within that order, what cannot be classified, what is left over, the remains, is what is new: it's what the mad are trying to say in spite of the repetitive compulsion. I analyzed this woman's delirium with this method. If you look, you will see that she repeats a number of formulas, but there is a series of phrases, of words that cannot be classified, that remain outside of this structure. I did that, and separated those words, and what was left?" Renzi said, lifting his face to look at old-man Luna. "Do you know what is left over? This phrase: The fat guy was waiting for her in the doorway and didn't see me and spoke to her about money and shone that hand that made her die. You see?" Renzi finished, triumphant. "The murderer is Almada, the fat guy."

Old-man Luna looked at him, impressed, and leaned over the paper.

"See?" Renzi insisted. "Notice how she says these words, underlined in red, she says them in the holes that can be made between what she is forced to repeat, the story of Bairoletto, the Virgin, and the whole delirium. If you look at the different versions, you will see that the only words that are in a different place are those with which she tries to tell what she saw."

"Hey, this is great. Did you learn this in college?"

"Don't screw around."

"I'm not screwing around, I'm serious. And now what are you going to do with all these papers? Your thesis?"

"What do you mean what am I going to do? We're going to print it in the newspaper."

Old-man Luna smiled as if he were in pain.

"Take it easy kid. Or do you think that this newspaper is dedicated to linguistics?"

"We have to print it, don't you see? That way Antúnez's lawyers can use it. Don't you see that the man is innocent."

"Listen to me, the guy is cooked, he doesn't have any lawyers, he's a pimp, he killed her because in the long run that's how those girls always end up. I think the little game with the words is phenomenal, but let's stop here. Do a fifty-line column telling how the broad was stabbed to death."

"Listen, Mr. Luna," Renzi cut him off. "That guy is going to spend what is left of his life in the joint."

"I know. But I've been in this business for thirty years and there is one thing I know: you have to avoid any problems with the police. If they tell you that the Virgin Mary killed him, you write that the Virgin Mary killed him."

"That's alright," Renzi said, gathering the papers. "In that case I will send the papers to the judge."

"Tell me, do you want to ruin your life? A madwoman as a witness to save a small-time pimp? Why do you want to get involved?" A sweet peacefulness shone upon his face, a calm that he had never seen. "Look, take the day off, go to the movies, do whatever you want, but don't make trouble. If you get mixed up with the police, I'll fire you from the newspaper."

Renzi sat down in front of the typewriter and put in a blank piece of paper. He was going to draw up his resignation; he was going to write a letter to the judge. Through the windows the city's lights looked like cracks in the darkness. He lit a cigarette and sat still, thinking about Almada, about Larry, hearing the madwoman talking about Bairoletto. Then he lowered his face and began writing almost without thinking, as if someone were dictating to him:

Fat, diffused, melancholy, the fil-à-fil Nile-green suit floating on his body, Almada went out with an air of secret euphoria to try to erase his dejection.

THE PRICE OF LOVE

for Andrés Rivera

He entered the hallway under the soft clarity of the late afternoon: imperturbable, donning a hat, a bit ridiculous; as if he were disguised, making an effort to look older or more self-assured, less frail than he was, with his twenty-second birthday recently celebrated, and a little package wrapped in tissue paper. He recognized the smell of humidity and burnt wood that came down through the air shaft, a pale invisible haze that he always associated with Adela's skin. In the elevator he looked at his face in the mirror, satisfied; then he got off, slow and dark, going over what he had prepared to say when they opened the door. They took a while to answer; he stood motionless, sideways to the door of the apartment, with a humble posture, afraid that if he insisted they would not receive him. From the other side came a moan that was barely perceptible, as if someone were praying in a low voice or crying under water. "It sounds like a cat meowing," he thought, "a cat with her young." He rang again; after a while the door opened slightly. At the door a girl who could not have been more than six years old was looking at him, her head bent to one side, with a timid expression that made her look like a bird. She wore little braids and glasses with thin lenses, which gave her an adult, concentrated expression. He crouched down to the girl's height.

"How are you?" he said to her. "Huh? Lucía."

The girl continued to look at him in silence, distant, detached.

"Mom isn't here," she said finally, as if she were reciting. "And I can't open the door to strangers."

"What do you mean, you don't remember me! Don't you remember Esteban?"

The girl shook her head no and stood still against the sun's glare, bright at the end of the hallway. "The same face, but aged prematurely," he thought, "as if the girl grew older instead of the mother."

"I was playing with him," the girl said suddenly, and showed him a rubber doll.

"Pretty."

"No, he's not pretty, the thing is that he floats."

"You don't say."

"In the bathtub, I put him in and he floats."

"So you put him in the bathtub and he floats," he said, and felt a little dumb talking to the girl down there. She was looking straight at him now, her eyes very pale, her myopic look thankful and turbid behind the lenses.

"And who are you?" she said then.

"I told you. I'm Esteban. What do you mean, you don't remember me?"

The girl adjusted her glasses and touched her face softly with her fingertips.

"Do you know what his name is?" she said, showing him the doll. "His name is Oscar."

"Very good. Now listen: did Adela tell you where she was going?"

"She won't be back."

"Why won't she be back?"

"She always leaves and then doesn't come back."

"She's inside. She's in bed with some guy," he thought, and felt a kind of happiness, as if that had been what he had come for. "Her with some guy and the girl playing with water."

"Okay," he said. "I'll come in, I'll wait for her."

The girl squeezed the doll against her body; it seemed like she was going to start crying, but she moved aside, leaving the door open.

Inside, the afternoon light was settling, dim against the twill curtains. Everything was the same as before, the things in their usual place, but there was no sign of Adela. "Women," he thought, trying to gain confidence. "Dirty, open. They bleed and they cry. Women," he thought, as if he were dreaming. He looked for an armchair and sat down in the middle of the room, his hat resting on his knees, covering the little pink-colored package. The girl had sat in front of him in a low chair, cradling the doll. "She looks like a somnambulist," he thought without any emotion, "a miniature version of the woman she is to become. Dumb, myopic, disenchanted."

"You were a boyfriend of mom's?"

"Yes," he said. "Now you remember?"

"I thought so," the girl said, and smiled at him, timid, peaceful.

He lit a cigarette and decided he would stay. He did not have anywhere to go, deep down everything was the same to him. "Wait here, wait somewhere else."

"You know," the girl said suddenly, "I know how to sing songs."

"You don't say?"

"Do you want to see?" she said, and adjusted her glasses before starting to sing in a low and serene voice, always with the same indifferent expression on her face:

> Oh Mother my mother
> oh joy of the altar
> shelter me and guide me
> to the celestial world

The girl sang, rigid in the chair. And then she stopped, abruptly.

"Very good," he said. "It's terrific how you sing. Who taught you?"

"Adela," the girl said, and became quiet once again.

The muffled rumble of the city came in through the window like a respiration, a gasp. Esteban felt that the smell in that place made him sad. It was a sweet smell, of orange juice, of damp earth, that forced him to think of his childhood, of the train rides to Bolívar sitting in the dining car. The girl had gotten off the chair and was playing in a corner. He heard her murmur and laugh, talking to herself. He got up and walked to the window. From there one could see the roofs and terraces of Buenos Aires. Sheet metal, skeletal boxes, television antennas. "Shitty city," he thought, "dirty and ruined."

When he looked back inside the girl was crouched down in a corner; she seemed to be smelling out the air, her face raised toward the noise that the woman's heels made on the floor tiles in the hallway. "There she is," he thought, hardened, defiant. "There she is," and he tried to find a phrase with which to receive her: "It's me. It's Esteban, I was nearby, and I wanted to see you. I was nearby, passing by, I felt like seeing you. I was nearby," he thought, as if praying, while the woman opened the door; her tall, soft figure outlined against the afternoon's last light.

"My love," Adela said, picking up the girl. "What does my little beauty have to say?"

"A gentleman is here," the girl said. Adela looked toward the far end of the room, blinded, for the blurred shape of the man who was smiling rigidly.

"Esteban," she said, flustered. "My dear."

"I was passing by. I came to see you," he said. "The girl was alone and I...."

"But yes, of course. Let me get myself together. My God, look how you've found me. But sit down, don't stand there like that, sit down, please."

"I was passing by," he persisted. "I felt like seeing you."

"Mom," the girl said, "is he your boyfriend?"

"It's Esteban," she said. "Esteban. But come here, my God, look how you are. She spends her life playing with water. Wait for me one minute, one minute and I'll be right with you."

Esteban watched her hug the girl and go to the other room, hurried and a bit guilty, like she always was when she dealt with her daughter. Then he heard them talking, he heard the sound of papers, the sound of water in the pipes; he sat still, without thinking, until Adela reappeared, smiling, her moist eyes shining faintly with misgiving. She had touched up her face; the fine wrinkles that lined her skin gave her a fatigued, unsettled expression.

"You're the same," he said. "Everything is the same."

"Get out of here. Go on. If you had only seen me today," she said. "Running from one place to another the whole damned day."

They looked at each other without talking, dissolved in the liquid clarity of the room.

"It's so strange," she said, and tried to smile. "I don't know what to say to you."

"Strange? What?"

"I don't know. That you came here, that I arrived and you…. But don't mind me."

"I was passing by, I tell you," he said, and moved slightly to one side. "I brought you this," he said, and began to carefully unwrap the package, trying not to ruin the clear paper with the little colorful flowers. "It's perfume. I brought you perfume. Do you like it?"

"It's so ridiculous, my God. He brings me perfume," she thought. "So beautiful. He makes me feel so old."

"Won't you open it?" he said. "Open it. Don't you want it? If you don't like it I can exchange it."

"No. Yes. Thank you," she said, and forced herself to smell the common perfume and be touched.

"It's imported," he said. "I can get smuggled perfume. All I want."

"Really?"

"I have a friend in customs," he said, always serious and solemn. "I can get what I want: perfume, fine clothes. If you want any of these things all you have to do is tell me."

She lifted her sharp, pale face avidly, trying to look fortunate, humble.

"It makes me so happy that you came. All this time, always thinking. If you could've seen me. First I found out you were living with Adolfo. You must be crazy, living with that guy, only you would think of it. I ran into him one day, didn't he tell you?"

"I lived, yes, in his house, for a time. At the end I got fed up: going on all day about politics. He's a Samaritan, a Salvation Army guy. Now I'm in a hotel."

"I was about to go see you, you know? Did Adolfo tell you? I want to tell you, look: I was so mean, that day. I want to apologize, Esteban. I was so nervous, I was unfair with you, I was nearly crazy."

"It's okay," he said. "It's not the first time that I've gotten thrown out of a place."

"No," she said, her head lowered, playing with her pearl necklace. "If you could see, my dear. I felt—"

"I know," he cut her off. "Don't get worked up over it."

"It's just that I have to tell you, I want you to know: I was nearly crazy, I was... nervous, neurasthenic."

"It's okay," he said. "Why don't you make some coffee."

"But of course. Look, see how I am. I just leave you there, my dear. I'll bring you something to eat. Do you want anything to eat? With the coffee?"

He stayed behind watching Adela's slender, elegant figure wrapped in the blue dress; the bluish glow of the woman's flesh walking toward the kitchen, her heels clicking on the floor. From the other room came a stifled laugh from the girl, who was playing, talking to herself.

"This girl is a saint, did you notice?" she said, looking back from the kitchen. "If you could see how she stays all alone, if you could see how she keeps me company."

Without motive, as if wanting to prepare her for what was coming, he forced himself to lie.

"She knew me perfectly, as soon as she saw me, your daughter did. She remembered a time I took her to the zoo."

"But of course, why wouldn't she remember? She hasn't stopped talking about you since you left."

"Good," he thought. "We're starting the games, her and I."

"But what have you done this whole time," she said, entering with the tray, without looking at him. "Tell me. What could you have been doing? You animal."

"A little of everything."

"I could kill you...you. You're an animal," she said, arranging the cups on the low coffee table. "I have strudel. Do you like strudel?"

"Yes, of course," he said, and began eating, bent over, throwing his body forward. "I saw you, one day. You were with some guy. Didn't you see me?"

"No," she said. "When?"

"Strange. You were on Suipacha, with the guy. Strange that you didn't see me. You were wearing a red dress, you looked all happy. I don't know why I thought the guy was Brazilian."

"Brazilian? You're so crazy. No. I'm sure it was, I remember now, I'm sure it was Patricia's friend, who—"

"I don't know why I thought the guy was Brazilian," he interrupted her. "One has those things, no? The way he walked, I suppose."

"I'm telling you, he was a friend of Patricia's, we must have been going to her house. But what does that matter now? It doesn't matter at all. Now you've come, you're here. I'm so happy. I would have never dared to look for you. You know me, you know how I am. I would have never dared, but since that day, you won't believe me, I was sure you would return. That we would meet to talk, so I could say, Esteban, my dear," she said, and it looked like her skin was cracking, dissolved in the pity she felt for herself. "I have missed you so much. I was crazy, as if I was empty. You'll never know," she said, and leaned over so close that Esteban was able to smell the sweet perfume that the woman gave off. It was a perfume like a turbid cloud that saddened him and made him decide, finally, to start to tell her why he had come.

"Yes, of course. But I, you know," he said, unable to look at her. "I want to tell you, I came to say goodbye. I'm going back to Bolívar."

"My God," she said. "You're crazy."

"Why? I want a change of scenery. My old man is going to put me in charge of the store. A guaranteed future," he said. "Buenos Aires is not for me. While I was with you I didn't realize it. Of course, since you used to lie to me."

"Esteban, please. I told you that that day, I told you that I..."

"No. But you're right. You're a practical woman. Your things will always go well. You get by."

"I get accustomed to things, you mean."

"That could be. But I don't, you see. I never get accustomed to things, I'll never get accustomed to anything. Those that do, it's like they're dead."

She searched for a cigarette and lit it, crouched over, trying to hide her shaking hands.

"And why are you going back, if I may ask?"

"Because you think things are a certain way and then everything turns out different. It seemed easy, didn't it, when I'd just arrived. I remember and it still makes me laugh. I was going to take the world by storm, just imagine, and there you have it." He stopped as if he could not breathe. "In this shitty city, do you realize? You get here, you think that everyone is waiting for you. When you want to stop and look around, you're lost, crushed."

Darkness moved in little by little; in the window the city was a gray bulk.

"And when are you thinking of leaving?"

"I don't know yet. Tomorrow, the day after. The worst thing will be when I get there. There are such sons of bitches in the small towns, you can't imagine. Every time someone returns, they throw a party."

Adela tried to calm herself; she smoked quietly, the smoke clouding her face.

"What do you think?"

"Nothing. I'm trying to understand."

"It's for the best, in the long run," he said, and got up. He walked to the window. At the very end the river was a dirty stain. "You still have the statue," he said, and lifted it with both hands. It was a silver figurine. The image of a virgin with the face of a bird. "Cuzco. Three hundred years. I never liked this statue, I have to confess. Too expensive for a house decoration. I always thought you were like this statue: too refined for me."

She sat still, her hands loose; she watched him place the statuette softly on the shelf and return to the couch.

"The guy who was with you had a really stupid-looking face," he said. "You like to collect. Men, I mean."

"Don't be a fool."

"But it's what you do."

"Okay, so what?"

"Nothing," he said.

He had sat down again and was looking at the floor, at one spot on the floor, concentrated, rancorous.

"Fool," she said. "You're such a fool."

She stretched out her hand and grazed his face with her fingertips. He looked at her straight on, indecisive, as if he didn't see her.

"What happened to us, Adela?"

"Who knows?" she said.

"I always remember when you arrived from Chile. I remember that, I don't know why. You were so beautiful. We were going to love each other our whole lives."

"Yes," she said. "We were going to love each other our whole lives."

"You brought me a bottle of pisco, do you remember, when you came from Chile," he said. "You'll never know how much I loved you. I wanted to marry you so you wouldn't be able to leave me. Tell me if I'm not a dumb shit."

"No," she said. "My dear."

"I'm so screwed up," he said, and sank his face into the woman's body.

"My love," she said, and hugged him. "My little one."

He had laid down on the sofa and was caressing her, his eyes closed, his face tense. She felt his hands against her body, touching her thighs lightly, where her thighs met, and she let herself be undone, wet, open.

"Did you see the perfume I brought you. I can get all I want," he said suddenly, still caressing her.

"Yes," she said. "Yes."

"I thought: with that I can get above water. The guy I told you about, the customs guy, tells me that with some cash I can set up on my own."

"Please," she said. "Don't talk now, wait, don't talk, please."

"Everything I need, at the most, is 100,000 pesos."

She felt weak. Dissolved. She felt she was drowning.

"No," she said. "No. Let me go," she said.

"What are you doing?" he said. "What's wrong?"

Adela was standing before him, her eyelids quivering slightly.

"How much do you need? How much money do you want?" she said. "I'll give it to you. If you come here, I'll give you the money. Is that good?"

"But, what's wrong?" he said, sitting awkwardly on the sofa, trying to smile. "Are you crazy?"

"You came for that, didn't you? You bring all your stuff, I'll give you the money."

Esteban got up slowly, until he was facing the woman.

"Why do you humiliate me?" he said.

"Who?" she said. "Who?"

"You. Why do you humiliate me? What are you looking for? Why do you humiliate me? Do you want to see me on the ground, on my knees? Is that what you want?" he said, and kneeled at the woman's feet. "There you go," he said. "Good. The lady is a lady. She has practical sense, she's proud, she has a sense of opportunity. The lady," he said.

"Get up, please. Don't be ridiculous."

"Ridiculous? Of course I'm ridiculous. Ridiculous. And? What of it?"

"Stop it. Don't ruin everything."

"Of course I'll ruin everything. I have no way out, I don't have anywhere to go. For you it's easy!"

The girl had laid back against the door frame and was watching them.

"Esteban, the girl," Adela said. "I ask you..."

He sought out the girl's face and smiled at her; then he opened his arms and began singing:

> Oh Mother my mother
> oh joy of the altar
> shelter me and guide me
> to the celestial world

He sang out of tune.

The girl was smiling at him, her face softened, squeezing the doll against her body, while Adela was hugging her in order to lift her up.

"She's going to be like you," he said. "Just like you: myopic, dumb."

"Leave," she said. "You're leaving."

"Okay," he said, and began to get up. "You're right."

In the other room the air was still clear and transparent, luminous against the white walls.

"What's wrong with him," Lucía asks.

"Nothing," Adela says. "Don't worry."

Kneeling down, she fixes the girl's hair, runs her hand over the girl's face, trying not to cry. From there, as if he were shrouded in a mist, distant in the semi-darkness of the other room, she sees Esteban hide the silver statue clumsily underneath his coat.

"Why was he singing?" the girl says.

"It doesn't matter," Adela says, and hugs her. "It doesn't matter, my dear. Mom will be right back."

When she goes out, he is still in the same place, with his overcoat buttoned up, his hat in his hand, an arm pressed against his body.

"You're leaving?" she says.

"I'm leaving," he says.

Adela watches him adjust the brim of his hat with one hand and walk slowly toward the door.

"Esteban," she says.

He turns around, pale, tense.

"I feel so sorry for you," she says.

"Yes," he says. "Yes. I know."

She watches the door close and stands still, her hands loose. On the other side of the window night has already fallen: the soft lights of the city shine in the darkness.

"Did he leave?" the girl says.

"Yes. He left," Adela says. "But he'll be back. Tomorrow he'll be back."

ASSUMED NAME

Homage to Roberto Arlt

for Josefina Ludmer

What I am writing here is a report, or better yet an abstract: at issue is the ownership of a text by Roberto Arlt, so I will try to be orderly and objective. I am the one who discovered the only story of Arlt's that has remained unpublished after his death. The text is called "Luba." Arlt wrote it approximately between March 25 and April 6, 1942. That is to say, shortly before his death. The text was written by hand, in a school notebook, with tight writing that covers the margins. "Luba" is the most important piece of a collection of unpublished writings by Roberto Arlt that I began to compile at the beginning of 1972. It was the thirtieth anniversary of his death, and I was placed in charge of preparing a publication in homage. The idea was to publish a volume that would include:

1. The texts published in newspapers and magazines but not collected in books. This section would comprise:
a) A narrative article entitled "The Occult Sciences in the City of Buenos Aires," which appeared in the newspaper *Tribuna Libre*, in Buenos Aires on January 28, 1920. It is the first piece published by Arlt, who at the time was twenty years old.
b) A chapter of *The Furious Toy*, published in March of 1925

in the magazine *Proa* (Year IV, N° 6), entitled "The Parochial Poet." This story, which recounts the meeting of Silvio Astier with a mediocre but successful poet, was transformed in the final version of the novel into the meeting with Timoteo Souza, "expert in theosophical arts."

c) Five "Etchings" of the series that Arlt published in the morning newspaper *El Mundo,* and which were not collected in a book. The texts are: 1. An Andalusian Dog. 2. The Uselessness of Books. 3. The Terrible Sincerity. 4. Geniuses of Buenos Aires. 5. Funeral Happiness.

d) *Fierce Separation,* a play in one act, which appeared in the newspaper *El Litoral,* in Santa Fe, on August 18, 1938. It deals with a grotesque scene in which a man who decides to commit suicide says good-bye to his wife and discusses his will with her.

2. The entirety of his unpublished writings:

a) An autobiographical story, sent by Roberto Arlt around 1939 to his editor Esteban Moied, which was to serve as a prologue to a new edition of a single volume containing *The Seven Madmen* and *The Flamethrowers.* The text was not used afterward and remained in the possession of Moied.[1]

---

[1]*Arlt's text reads as follows*: "I have the bad taste of being super enchanted to be Roberto Arlt. My mother, who read romance novels, added on to Roberto the name Godofredo, which I do not use even in jest, and everything because of reading *Jerusalem Delivered* by Torquato Tasso. It is true that I would prefer being named Pierpont Morgan or Henry Ford or Edison or Charles Baudelaire, but in the physical impossibility of transforming myself according to my taste, I opt for becoming accustomed to my last name. Is it not perhaps an elegant last name, substantial, worthy of a count or a baron? Is it not worthy of appearing in a bronze piece in one of those strange machines, which display the sum total of the *Many-Sided Machine of Roberto Arlt*, and which work when one feeds it a coin?

"On the other hand, I have an unbreakable faith in my future as a writer. I have compared myself with almost everyone in the scene; I have seen that all these good people have an esthetic or human concern, not for themselves, but for others. This kind of generosity is so fatal for the writer, in the way that it would be fatal for a man who wished to make a fortune to be as honorable with the goods of others as with his own. I believe that in this I have the advantage over all the others. I am a perfect egoist. I do not give a damn for the happiness of man or mankind. The problem of my happiness, however, interests me enormously. Here writers live more or less happily. Nobody has any problems other than the silliness as to whether they should rhyme or not. Everyone lives

b) Notes for a novel in preparation, outlines, ideas, and literary anecdotes written by Arlt between March 2 and 30, 1942, in a forty-page, 17 x 21.5 cm San Martín notebook. c) "Luba," the story to which I have referred, written in that same notebook, from which eighteen pages were torn out. The pages, numbered 41 to 75, were attached with a paper clip.

To gather these materials I spent long afternoons in the National Library examining newspapers and magazines of the time, maintained a correspondence, and interviewed friends and acquaintances of Roberto Arlt. Finally, I placed several notices in newspapers in Buenos Aires and in the interior announcing my intention to buy any unpublished material by Arlt which could be preserved. Through this medium (besides the autobiographical portrait and a dozen letters)[2] I obtained the notebook in which Arlt wrote almost daily during March of 1942.

One morning, an older man, timid and affable, brought it to me; he was a retired railroad worker and his name was Andrés Martina. He had been the director of a socialist library in Bánfield during the '30s; there he met Roberto Arlt. Toward the end of 1941 Arlt rented a large shed outside his house in Lanús and installed a lab where he experimented with his invention of starched stockings. At that time, as Martina confirmed to me, Arlt had associated himself with the actor Pascual Nacaratti to commercially operate the indus-

---

such a tepid existence, then, that an individual who has just a little imagination ends up by saying to himself: 'Argentina is the land of milk and honey.' The first one to do a little psychology and a few strange things, will have those people in their pockets.

"In our time, the writer believes he is the center of the world. He bullshits all he wants. He deceives public opinion, consciously or unconsciously. People who even undergo difficulties in writing their family, believe that the mentality of the writer is superior to that of his fellow man. All of us, those who write and sign our names, do it to make ends meet. Nothing else. And to make ends meet we do not hesitate in affirming that white is black and vice-versa. People are looking for the truth and we give them counterfeit money. It is the trade, the 'métier.' People believe they receive legitimate merchandise and they believe it is prime material, when it merely entails a base falsification, of other falsifications, which were also inspired by falsifications."

[2]   The letters, numbered 12, 14, 15, 16, 21, 27, 43, 39, 40, 41, 45, were included in Roberto Arlt's *Correspondence*, Selection, Prologue and Notes by Emilio Renzi, Buenos Aires: Editorial Tiempo Contemporáneo, 1973.

trial production of the stockings. They had founded an enterprise (Arna): Nacaratti was in charge of looking for credit and Arlt acted as the industrial partner. According to Martina, Arlt arrived every morning and locked himself in the lab well into the night. He had installed an autoclave, a barometer, a duralumin leg, and other artifacts conceived by him. He worked with rubber latex, searching for a solution that would preserve the softness of the stockings.

"I had gotten enthusiastic with the crazy guy. He was capable of convincing anybody that he would be successful. You had to see him inside that shed, dying of heat, wrapped in an imitation-leather apron, smoking nonstop and speaking to himself. He worked with solutions of benzoic rubber, feeding his autoclave up to 120 degrees, manipulating all those apparatuses at the same time; the place looked like the engine room of a steamer. He didn't think of anything else. When the business took off he was going to buy me a trip to Spain," the old man said, smiling behind his clear eyes. "I ended up loving him like a son. One day an oxygen tube exploded on him, he was almost burned alive. I remember that he appeared in the kitchen of my house, his face with soot, his eyebrows singed, dejected and humble. They had already evicted him from two or three places, because of the explosions. 'Don't worry,' I tell him. 'Continue right ahead, go ahead even if the whole house burns down.' Then the man starts to cry and hugs me, grateful that I should have confidence in him."

Arlt was going to the lab in Lanús almost every day, between February and June of 1942.

"He had gotten used to coming to see me before leaving, and he spoke to me about everything he was going to do with the money he'd make. He had such ideas." The old man became quiet, as if he were thinking. "The last time I saw him he says, 'I'm missing just one detail.' Just one detail, do you realize? He died convinced. Now whether that invention was going to work or not, nobody knows. He took the secret to the grave, he had created it all by himself. 'I'm missing just one detail,' he'd say, who knows which one it was."

After Arlt died, the lab remained in the hands of Martínez, without anybody showing up to remove the things. He had found the notebook in a trunk; until I became interested in it, no one had bothered to investigate if it was valuable.

"There are piles of notes about a novel: he was writing it or thought about writing it around that time. Sometimes he spoke to me, he had taken the story from an article about some crime. A guy who had poisoned his wife."

He handed me the neatly-wrapped notebook; he did not want to accept the money I offered him.

"Maybe by searching something else will appear. I'll go see," he told me.

"Go look," I told him, anxious to inspect the manuscript. "If you find something bring it to me, don't talk to anyone else."

1

The notebook is numbered from 1 to 80: the central pages (from 41 to 77) have been ripped out. The outline and plan of a novel are found in the first thirty pages. It is the story of a small-time Borgia, a sickly, genial murderer who plots a perfect crime. I transcribe the notes here according to their order in the manuscript.

A man, awake, thinks well of another and trusts him completely, but he is troubled by dreams in which his friend acts as a mortal enemy. It is revealed at the end that the dreamed personality is the real one. (Amid a crowd, in the jungle of a city, imagine a man whose fate and life are in the other's power, as if the two were in a desert.)

Lettif: a youth, pure. (Hamlet + Mishkin + Luis Castruccio.)[3] Rinaldi finds him in a smallish cafe on Leandro Alem. He begins to guide him. (The criminal education.) He initiates him. The greatest spiritual passions come upon them. Rinaldi knows how to activate his

---

[3] Lettif seems to be vaguely inspired by Luis Castruccio. This criminal, famous in turn-of-the-century Buenos Aires, planned the perfect crime which would make him loaded with money: he murdered Alberto Bouchot, a Frenchman by origin and without family, whom he had previously hired as a servant, to collect the insurance. Discovered, condemned to death, he was pardoned; he died a madman, confined in the Asylum of Our Lady of Mercy. He devoted the last five years of his life to writing letters to the president of the Republic, Carlos Pellegrini, to inform him of his innocence. When he died, more than 5,000 letters—in which, with slight variations, he repeated the same thing—were found in a hole that he had made in the wall of his wing of the asylum.

fantasy. Transformations. (An earthly *Faust*.)

Rinaldi speaks to him for the first time about the beauty of crime. Tendency toward unlimited control and faith in authority. He is happy to feel that power. He goes into debt. Better yet: Rinaldi insists on lending him money. The debt grows. Disproportionate pride and struggle against clarity.

The economic debt as a tie of blood. Rinaldi makes the idea of crime enter that virgin mind. Not so much the idea of crime, but rather the idea of a natural barter between death and money. He speaks to him about life insurance. Collected for the death of an other. Capitalism speculates on good sentiments. The steps must be: Rinaldi "forces" him to go into debt (generosity). He begins to corrupt him; finally he submits him to Matilde. He accepts living with a prostitute to protect her from the police. There is never sexual intercourse. She wants to adopt a girl. Lettif becomes enthusiastic. They put a notice in the newspaper. (Chapter where the families who come to deliver their children parade before them. "Then your son will stay with us?" "Yes, sir." "And if I turn out to be a pervert, a bastard?" etc.) They choose an eight-year-old girl (María), beautiful, lame.

Then comes an outline of Rinaldi.

Fat, gasping, the fil-à-fil Nile-green suit stained with coffee, chalk, and lipstick. The bar in shadows, the fans with wooden blades. Sitting always at the same table, his face full of scars, the skin worn out. Up close he looks like a frog, metallic eyes.

"What is robbing a bank compared with founding it?" he says, and breaks into laughter. (It's true, that's how he talks: *What is*— gasp—*robbing*—gasp—*a bank*—gasp—*compared with*—gasp— *founding it.*) He always finds him anytime he goes there.

"Do you believe it's easier to be a bookkeeper than an apostle in a religion? How naive! What evangelist did they stick in a closet as a youth to count money that was not his, nor for him?" He stops to breathe, passes a dirty handkerchief across his neck, and sinks his face into a bottle of beer, then keeps talking with his asthmatic gasping.

"What saint did they bury in a basement and force to go blind over columns of figures and eight daily hours every day of his existence? What devout person did they force to travel hanging like a gorilla from the handles of a bus four times daily every day of his life? To what angel did they weave *in vitam* the victories of the etamine in which he dressed?"

Lettif decides to kill María to collect the life insurance. He buys the arsenic before taking out the policy. He goes with Matilde, they take out policies for the two of them. But there his design fails: the insurance companies refuse to underwrite a policy in his favor for the death of a girl. "They consider the insurance carried out on the life of a child immoral." So he decides to kill Matilde.

The principal sense of the first part must be: instinctive consciousness of superiority. Insatiability of the plan (geometry). The fundamental thing is that he is convinced that everything is of an absolute simplicity. He looks always for a solid point of support (Rinaldi's "fatness"). A man out of the ordinary. He cannot stand the debt; but he is incapable of working. Or better yet, he doesn't have the vaguest idea that who he is destined to be and that for which he is chosen prevents him from accumulating wealth. (His strangeness consists entirely of being unable to earn money, "a madman.") The doubt will dissipate when in the zeal of securing the money for himself, he loses it.[4]

Then comes a sketch of Lettif, written by Arlt, forging the style of a psychiatric report.

"The Man of Prey" (include as a chapter before the trial). The murderer, whose anthropometric mensuration we have been unable to obtain, is a man of thirty years, of short height, delicate and fair face, completely beardless, with straight blond hair, light blue eyes that rarely look straight at you, an extraordinarily large and round head, triangular and vampiric ears, pronounced frontal bones. He smiles

---

[4] The last five lines have been added in pencil in the manuscript.

constantly, lowers his eyes and blushes with excessive ease. In the middle of his forehead a very marked protuberance is present, which he attributes to a blow received in infancy. Born into the lower social classes and for many years a servant, he has been able to raise himself due to a relative instruction which seems to have done him great harm, turned all of his notions upside down. A big fan of eighteenth-century philosophers, he floats intellectually between dementia and genius (see his *Treaty on Poison*). (Better yet: *Eulogy of Arsenic*), constituting one of the most characteristic models of that type which Lombroso calls "mattoid," and which we will denominate as "crazy" to give an approximate translation. In 1924—at the age of twenty-one—he decided to commit suicide; he thus states in a holographic will drawn up on sealed paper, which was found in his home. This document is palpable proof of the mental imbalance of its author. He starts by bequeathing his possessions to the Italian Hospital, with the condition that they not be employed in the maintenance of the women's room, who are, in his judgment, extremely prejudicial and unpleasant beings. He continues with a profession of religious faith in which he declares himself an atheist; he states that the only hell is not the one described by "the charlatan from the Vatican," but rather the central fire that will be worse for the living than for the dead, which "lifts the earth from the depths of the ocean without caring about (to say it as such) the lives of the sailors"; he proclaims that astronomy is the base and foundation of all the sciences; he concludes with a long transcription from Flammarion and a speech by Victor Hugo about nonreligious teachings. The will was found inside an envelope that read: "Null until further resolution." The author did not think that if the cover were removed, the nullity would disappear.

Written on top of the page we find the title: Criminal Education. *Further down, another title*: The Criminal in the Brick Jungle.

The notes continue on the following page.

He learns them all in secret. By himself, he wants to prepare himself for everything. He becomes horribly enthusiastic about something (for example with *Hamlet*).

His father punished him brutally on his head. "I did not cry but I wanted to kill him." Or better yet: "So as not to cry I thought how I could kill him without being (...) ever."[5] Unsociable. Taciturn. He looks at all children as if looking at something strange, whose good and perverse parts he discovered long ago. Sickly "passion"—corresponding—for little María (12 years old).

Only doubt: to accumulate wealth "scientifically."[6] His discoveries in astronomy.

The greatest bodily passions come upon him. The effect of vice: its horror and its cruelty. He despises lies with all his strength. He believes. Otherwise: nothing. The unbeliever will appear for the first time in a horrible episode and already in jail. The little, lame María (12 years old). He fondles her in the visiting hallway. "Don't kill me, uncle," she says in a low voice, trying to protect him, to keep the prison guards from hearing her.

Part II. The decision taken, Lettif only needs to carry out the second part of his plan. To decide on the poison he spends the afternoons studying in the National Library all the treaties on toxicology that fall into his hands. (He writes an essay: *Eulogy of Arsenic*.) He falsified a prescription and on July 18 he obtained 20 grams of lethal dust (Rinaldi helps him falsify the prescription).

Written in the margin it reads: Rinaldi is the one who falsifies the prescription. Theory about the ease of imitating—forging—handwriting. (The same as Kostia) Graphology: he changes the writing and he changes fate. Examples: imitate Napoleon's hand-writing, copy the traits of his writing to acquire his character.

---

5   There is a word crossed out (maybe "discovered" or "described"); another is added on top of it; it is illegible.

6   The manuscript is difficult to read. It could also be read as "cynically."

The notes continue with the development of the crime.

They begin to supply the toxic to Lisette.[7] (Keeps precise documentation of all his actions in a memo-book; starts to meticulously write the days and times in which he applies the poison.) He mixes the arsenic in his wife's food after having tried the toxic himself and confirmed that it did not have an intense smell or taste.

A chapter: Rinaldi enters the subway stop. Empty platform. A beggar sleeps flung out on a bench. He wakes her. "What's your name?" Rinaldi said as the subway was entering with a whistling. "Who?" the woman said. (Cracked, sunken face.) "You, damn it," Rinaldi gasped. "What's your name?" (The woman squeezed a kind of dark and muddy tunic, which covered her stained skin, tightly around herself with both hands.) "What's your name?" "Echevarre, María del Carmen," the woman said. "Here," Rinaldi said, and handed her a one hundred peso bill stuck to starched cloth. "Buy yourself a hat."

The woman looks at the bill close up, against her face, as if she were blind, and rocks in place without knowing what to do. When she realizes it truly is a hundred pesos she starts to let out a kind of moan with her mouth closed, like a child who cries in his sleep. Rinaldi majestically walks toward the subway and installs himself in the middle of the car, alone and erect, under the yellow light. When the subway takes off the woman tries to keep up, running beside it, facing Rinaldi; she waves to him with both hands, with a romantic look, while Rinaldi fades into the darkness. "Echevarre, María del Carmen," the woman repeats, alone in the empty platform, squeezing the bill with both hands, her eyes fixed on the darkness of the tunnel.

Three or four chapters further on: Lisette alone in a bar thinks that she wants to leave. "I'm going to grab the girl and I'm going to get on a train and I'm going to go anywhere," she thinks. She is seen traveling in the middle of the night, leaning against the illuminated window, the girl sleeping against her body. At that point the beggar shows up, asks her for money. Lisette refuses. "Give me money, girl,"

---

[7]   In the process of writing, as can be noted, Arlt has changed the name of the woman (Lisette for Matilde) and the age of the girl (first 8 years old, then 12).

the old woman said in profile, her hand stretched out. "Go away," Lisette said, and tried to push her, but the old woman grabbed her by the wrist and fell toward her. "You're lost, you. Cursed," she speaks to her slowly, in a low voice, leaning over her. "I'm a Gypsy. Queen and mother. Echevarre, María del Carmen," she made several signs with her free hand. "You were dying, you. You will die a contorted death. I'm the Gypsy," the old woman said and started to leave. Lisette becomes terrified, tries to catch up with her, offers her money, uselessly, etc. (The beggar = Cassandra.)

Henceforth Arlt's notes are focused on the crime.

Lettif will also write down, regularly, the medical visits that his wife receives during the course of her sickness, and which are attributed by the doctor to gastritis. (In a Penal Code he had conscientiously marked the articles relating to the process that must be observed in the cases of inhumations of people, when it is suspected that the death is due to a crime.)

Lisette's sickness and suffering make his love for her grow. He loves her as he has never loved anyone.

During that time he visits Rinaldi daily. Conversations (see): the core of Part II. Discussions about Nietzsche.

Part III. (From Lisette's death to the firing squad: trial.) The last day, when Lisette is already painfully struggling in the rasping breaths of agony, Lettif went up to his wife and (according to a subsequent story) contemplated her for an instant; after a small hesitation, he brought his hand to the moribund's twitching face and blocked her nose and mouth, asphyxiating her. When he confirmed that she was dead, he got into bed and covered his head with the bedclothes, like a frightened child. Half an hour later he was deep asleep. (Better to end the chapter with the scene of Lettif buried under the blankets.)

The following morning he again called the doctor, who expedited a certificate of death, diagnosing a cerebral blockage. (Chapter: Wake. Rinaldi, the girl, and Lettif alone. Lisette in the coffin, laid out: pale and beautiful. A whore comes and brings a bouquet of paper flowers.)

Before the corpse is retired from the room, Lettif, trapped by the inexorable mechanism of his plan, calls the insurance company to announce that his wife has died. Which leads to the informing of the director of the company in case they considered it necessary to confirm it in person. This ill-timed communication provokes suspicions. Autopsy.[8]

(One of the doctors observes that the autopsy proves that, in spite of the poisoning, the death must have occurred by asphyxiation. "Yes, doctor, it is true," Lettif says. "I killed her like Othello did Desdemona.")

Rinaldi (who is a lawyer) takes over the defense. "Philosophic" arguments: he founds the defense on Nietzsche. (Rinaldi: A half-drunk Polonius.)   Sanctity: the "juridical" precedent of Raskolnikov.

Lettif is condemned to death.   Surprised, he stands up and declares before the Tribunal:

"I cannot conceive of the death penalty being sought for a man who has failed in a commercial operation. Particularly keeping in mind that I committed it in my own house and upon the person of a foreigner, which is evidently extenuating. I must insist that if it deals with a foreigner the offense does not exist, and never by an Argentine. The deceased Lisette Armand was a French citizen; that surely is an extenuating circumstance that proves that I have not done harm to any Argentine. I have good precedents, it is the first time that I find myself imprisoned and I have had and have good conduct; they are, thus, extenuating circumstances. The medical assistance that I leant her during the agony, is extenuating. The good will that Lisette gave to the business of the insurance, which is a lawful business as a commercial act before the law, is another extenuation. She was my legal wife; that is another extenuation. The law requires criminal will for there to be an offense, and I did not have the will to kill, but rather that of

---

[8]   Crossed out can be read: "The judge orders that Lettif be present at the ceremony.   In the middle of the autopsy he takes his wife's hand and cries (end of chapter)."

obtaining money through a legal transaction; that is another extenuating circumstance. I wanted her to stop suffering; that is another. There are several other extenuations that I do not remember. The fact is that the sickness and the death occurred in my house; that is another extenuation."

In jail, Lettif keeps a diary. These notes must begin together with the story, I mean, they will be interspersed.

(Conclusion): He is executed by firing squad. They take him barefoot, in socks like Di Giovanni. At the time of execution, Lettif, turning toward the direction he names, says: "Good-bye North, good-bye South...East, West." Rinaldi and María—outside, on the other side of the walls—attend the execution. They walk hand in hand on the sidewalk. They hear the firing. Morning is breaking. They leave, walking through the empty city. In the middle of the street the madwoman (Echevarre) appears, walking with her arms open, alone against the sleeping city, talking in a low voice, as if praying. (End)

On page 29 of the notebook the outline of the novel per se ends. From that point on there are notes on Lettif's diary, ideas about the characters, writings, and reflections of Arlt himself.

(Lettif's Diary.) The night before I began my notes, I worked on them for four hours. It will be a document, a settling of accounts. No one will find these pages (under the boards of the bed). Rinaldi—my lawyer—will be in charge of taking them out. My crime is gentle, meditated, scientific. Even though my cause is somewhat delicate, I hope that I will not be condemned to more than ten years in jail, which I plan to take advantage of to study. She is dead and feels nothing; in as much, I have paid the policy and have lost two hundred and thirty pesos, including in this the costs of the doctor and the funeral.

I believe in the world of prison, in its reprobate customs. I accept living in it, like I would accept, if I were dead, living in a cemetery, as long as I lived in it like a true dead person.

Not to do anything clean nor hygienic: cleanliness and hygiene are not from this world. To feed on dreams. And to believe oneself truly imprisoned for all eternity. I did not feel surprised to discover the customs of the prisoners, those customs that make those men different from (at the margin of?) living ones: going around in circles inside the cell (12 steps). This same life I have carried out in secret out there. But now I am afraid.

In the library of the prison he reads Pascal. He thinks that "modern intelligence is in full confusion."

The death penalty. The criminal is killed because the crime uses up all the strength of a man to live. If he has killed, he has lived it all. He can already die. Murder is exhaustive.

Between Rinaldi and Lettif the same relationship as that between thought and dreams.

I read this in Melville: "How insincere, how inconceivable that an author—in any possible circumstance—could be frank with his readers."

Then comes a sketch of Rinaldi.

In spite of the fact that he had been sinking for at least fifteen years, Rinaldi managed to stay afloat, assisted by his title of lawyer. The piece of paper obtained after long years of idling about in dilapidated boarding houses and milk bars was his life preserver, the oxygen tent that allowed him to survive. Thanks to the title, they had put him in charge of the contracting office; he was responsible for arranging the placing of women for the variety shows of all of Latin America. Work certificates, sanitary controls, passports, everything had to run like clockwork so the women could move from one place to another, enter and leave the country without any problems.

Several illegible paragraphs follow and then it reads.

In the downward slope of Corrientes the city grows quiet,

submerged in a blue fog that the wind lifts against the bright signs. Rinaldi slides along sticking to the wall, head down, infuriated, holding the fine-brimmed hat with his right hand when the wind from the river hits him straight on. "Years that I've wanted to take off," he is thinking as he goes. "Set up on my own in Panama. Quito: Ecuador." He saw himself crossing the gangplank dressed in gray, with a pig-skin suitcase, holding the brim of his hat against the breeze off the port. "I have nothing to lose," he thought. "What can matter to me now?"

That text is the last reference to the project of the novel. Beginning on page 32 are the notes on anarchism.

The great purity of Kraskov's type of anarchism is that for him crime coincides with suicide (see again the book by Savino: *Memories of an Anarcho-Syndicalist*). A life is paid for with a life. Reasoning is false but economic. (That is to say: in this society, moral.)

Love letter: "If you don't come, I'll kill myself. I'll shoot myself a little above the heart in the secret hope of dying and of continuing to live long enough for you to arrive and see me."

Story of an anarchist who must infiltrate the police. Together with him: an informant who keeps his lists up to date. Names written in printed hand-writing. Various inks. Lines. Scratches. Numbers. (He does sums, averages.)

"My real biography is written in the dossier that the police keeps on me; everything about me that is worth remembering by mankind is kept in that file."
The revolutionary is a marked man. He does not have personal interests, nothing of his own; not even a name. Everything in him is subject to an exclusive interest, to only one passion: the revolutionary struggle. Is he not the best modern hero? (Macbeth + Don Quijote = Lenin.)

"Men like me are not afraid of death," he said. "It is an accident that makes us right."

P. Scarfó (letter to his sister, quoted by Androtti: *The Anarchists in Argentina*): "If the revolutionary masses erupted into my room set upon tearing to pieces the bust of Bakunin and destroying my library, I would fight against them to the end." An "Etching" could be made out of this. An extreme example of the same affair can be seen in a man like Maxim Gorky. Commenting on a conference of "rural indigents" held in Moscow in the year 1919 he indicates that "several hundred peasants were housed in the Romanov Winter Palace. When, once the conference had ended, these men left, it was seen that not just all of the bathrooms of the palace, but also an enormous number of the urns from Sèvres, from Saxony, and from the Orient had been employed as urinals. And not out of necessity, for the toilets were in order and the pipes were functioning. No, this vituperative event was the expression of the desire to ruin, to damage beautiful objects" (M. Gorky's *Days with Lenin*, p. 24). It does not even cross his mind that the peasants were acting, without knowing it, as art critics; that is to say, they *used* the urns from Sèvres. For Gorky the urns from Sèvres are only "beautiful objects," untouchable, that everyone must "recognize" and "respect." He does not realize that those men, by pissing in the urns from Sèvres, inside the Romanov Palace, are denying that beauty is universal; they are actually opposed to the bourgeois idea of a beauty that is more beautiful the less useful it is (when it is not useful for anything). By using them in such a "brutal" manner (so unesthetically) the peasants are looking at the "beautiful object" to know what purpose it serves. Beauty is untouchable: *it must be useless.* There is the entire crime: a crime against property (even if Gorky does not like it).

Immediately the idea for a story appears.

A theme: the pure man and the evil woman in an extreme situation. Enclosed: see how they change, transform (both stuck in jail?).

The man detained by the political police because he was lazy about taking care of the documents. He knew it, he didn't do it, etc.

Regarding the "Etching": "Are The Urns From Sèvres Any Good As Originals?"[9] Underneath what is narrated by Gorky one can see what kind of characters the Bolsheviks were: in 1919 they considered it the most natural thing in the world to house the Muzhik in the Romanov Palace (without removing, on the other hand, the urns).

María Kolugnaia. When she gains her freedom they accuse her of being a traitor. To restore herself she shoots an officer of the gendarmery. Condemned to forced labor she commits suicide to protest the corporal punishment inflicted upon a comrade.

Another about "The Urns." Trotsky (in his *Autobiography*) talking about 1918: "When the soldier, yesterday's slave, suddenly finds himself in a first-class car of a train and he rips off the velvet that covers the seats to make himself a pair of gaiters, even in such a destructive act, the awakening of personality is revealed. The ill-treated and trampled Russian peasant, accustomed to receiving slaps and the worst insults, found himself all of a sudden, perhaps for the first time in his life, in a first-class car; he sees the velvet vestments; inside his own boots he has foul-smelling rags; and he rips off the velvet, saying to himself that he too has a right to something better." It seems like a criticism of Gorky's comment. (Again: beauty is only valuable when one can answer what purpose it serves? How can it be used? *Who* can use it? There is no universal beauty.)

In Moscow, threatened by the White Army, to Lenin who decides to mobilize those condemned by common offenses:
"No, not with them."

---

[9]   As far as we know, Arlt never got to write this "Etching." In any case, these ideas about the character of the class of art and of esthetic taste are coupled with some concepts exposed in his essay "The Failed Writer." "Writers called universal have never been universal, but rather writers of a determinable class, admired and deified by the satisfactions they were capable of adding to the refinements which, in and of themselves, the class treasured as excellently acquired goods. Those below, the opaque masses, elastic and terrible, which lived fighting in the terrible struggle of the classes throughout the ages, did not exist for those geniuses" (in Roberto Arlt's *Novelas completas y cuentos*, Buenos Aires: Fabril, 1963, III, p. 239).

"For them," Lenin answered.

(Remember Simón Radowitski: they ship him to Ushuaia —
life imprisonment. Appalling conditions, bad food, piled up. He
stands up, shackled: "Fellow thieves and murderers," he says, and
calls for resistance to the world capitalist system.)
    I believe that the fierce servility and the inexorable cruelty of
men from this century will never be surpassed. I believe that we have
been given the mission of attending the twilight of piety and that we
are left without any solution other than to write furious outpourings so
that we will not go out to the streets to throw bombs or install brothels.

Next another note appears about the story "Luba."

    Until now he has been lucky: everything turns suddenly. Life
as a game of chance. The police after him. He has not slept in two
days. The walls are moving in. He decides to take refuge in a brothel.
(The woman: Luba.)
    Scene: Due to a random drawing he must execute an ex-
comrade who turned out to be an infiltrated policeman. Bullet to the
temple. (The Browning with eight shots.) He holds his forehead up
with the palm of his hand, like one holds a child. He calms him down.
"It's an instant," he says to him. "One doesn't feel anything." He
cries.
    Marcos Rodríguez, Spanish anarchist. Condemned to forced
labor in Ushuaia. He refuses to have his shackles removed during
Holy Week so as to look more like his Savior. Before, he went into
churches and fired his revolver at the crucifixes.
    Title: "Property is Theft."
    He says: "The law allowed me to get to know crime." (Better
yet: "Thanks to the law I was able to get to know evil" or sin.)
    Does anybody ever sleep between jail and the gallows?
    Balzac: "Illusion is a memory converted into desire."

Immediately following (end of page 40) is found the first

paragraph of the story that Arlt had started to write directly in the notebook.

He arrived too early: it was ten at night; but the grand white parlor with golden chairs and mirrors along the walls was already prepared to receive the visitors. All the lights were on. In a corner, near an almost dark drawing room, sitting next to each other, three young women were speaking in a low.[10]

The text is interrupted here: it entails the start of "Luba," but the pages have been torn out. Arlt's notes continue in the last four sheets (numbered from 77 to 80); they were written starting from the end, beginning on the back cover. The large part of these notes are entries and formulas about methods for the starched stockings.[11] Also seen are some sketches of machines and apparatuses, various drawings, and diagrams for a voltmeter. Together with these technical notes, some notes of Arlt's referring to literature also exist. They are the following:

I didn't plan on telling anyone: I kept the secret, like a suicidal person the jar of poison. But no one had arrived yet who could...
    I cannot think without writing.

---

[10]   *We have transcribed this paragraph as it appears in its definitive version in the original of the story. In the notebook, instead, respecting the variations that Arlt wrote without crossing anything out as he proceeded, the text reads as follows:* It was eleven ten at night: too early. He arrived too early: it was ten at night. The parlor with lights and covered with mirrors reflected the grand white parlor with golden chairs and mirrors along the walls where it was already prepared already prepared to receive the visitors. All the lights on were on. Sitting to one side, near the drawing room, the three women. To the side, near the the drawing room almost dark, three young women were sitting next to each other speaking.

[11]   *An example of the kind of notes might be this one: Mixing formula. Starched stockings.* Steel-tempering Vulcacized P. + Vulcacized 774; then add the already-prepared mixture, 10.5% V of Vulcanized Mercaptan — A good hot pure rubber mixture + 100% clear crêpe, sulfur 2; paraffin oil 2; 0.6 ozocerite; 0.8% active zinc oxide. Mercerize — saturate with this mixture, not too fast (careful!), then through a benzoate solution of Vulcanized 8 + 774. Put the solution through the autoclave.

To Kostia: defense of plagiarism. (Write everything: as it comes.) I write this to the young people who have not yet been corrupted like me, writing every day because I have given myself soul and life to this profession in which to make a living, I lose my soul. I still do not write "for the sake of writing" like so many others who, in spite of everything, cannot write.

To mold a masterpiece, to weave a tapestry that will last a century, it is necessary to feel, to think, and to write. We cannot think if we do not have time to read, nor feel if we find ourselves emotionally exhausted, we cannot write if we do not have free time (that is to say: money to finance free time). We cannot coordinate what we do not have.

In addition there is a squared off section with a list of books (read by Arlt in those days or which Arlt planned to buy): *Quantum Mechanics* by O. Asendorf. *Organic Chemistry* by L. Panunzio. *Manual of Economic Politics* by N. Bujarin. *Days with Lenin* by M. Gorky. *Bouvard and Pécuchet* by G. Flaubert. *The Dark* by L. Andreyev. *Anarchism in Argentina* by J. Androtti. *Almayer's Folly* by J. Conrad. *Irresponsable* by M. Podestá (next to this title Arlt had written in parenthesis: The man of magnets). *Within a Budding Grove* by M. Proust.

There were also monetary figures and sums. To Kostia: $2,000; to Reynald: $700; to Raúl, 600 plus 18,000. I owe: 33,000 (six months).

Arlt wrote in this notebook between March 3 and 27, 1942. To verify these dates and confirm the existence of the story "Luba," it is necessary to enumerate the papers that were found in between the pages of the notebook.

2

Between the pages of the notebook there was a letter and the account written by Arlt of the application for a patent for his invention of the starched stockings.[12] The original of this text reads as follows:

New industrial method to produce a stocking for women that does not run.

To date it has been attempted to avoid that the tearing of one thread in the stocking determine the destruction of the stocking by means of employing liquid-rubber products. These methods have not worked, for if the rubber solutions are too thick, they alter the esthetic aspects of the stocking, and if these solutions are too liquid, they lack the adhesive consistency to prevent the loosening of a thread which then tears. This problem has acquired so much importance that they are presently making small sawing machines, destined solely to repair the accident of "the run." The author of this application—Roberto Godofredo Arlt, born in Buenos Aires on April 2, 1900—has resolved the stated problem by coating the internal surface of the stocking with a film of solid rubber, sufficiently thin as to be transparent like the stocking whose destruction we are trying to avoid. To this end he has invented a method for which he solicits a patent.

The letter (and this was the key to my investigation) had been received by Arlt in those days and confirms the existence of the story. Typewritten, it was sent by a certain Saúl Kostia[13] and it reads as follows:

Adrogué, April of 1942

It is hot and raining here. I love these hazy days, these moist,

[12]   The patent was granted to Arlt on April 10, 1942; it carries the number 12,365 (see *Register of Intellectual Property, Inventions and Derivations, and Related Items*, V. II, 1942, First Semester).

[13]   Juan Carlos Onetti makes reference to Kostia in his portrait of Roberto Arlt, which served as the prologue to the Italian translation of *The Seven Madmen*. He says: "Then I knew that Kostia was an old friend of Arlt's, that he had grown up with him in Flores, a Buenos Aires neighborhood, that he had probably participated in the first adventures of *The Furious Toy*." Before, he had indicated: "Kostia, to the limit of intimacy which he imposed, is one of the most intelligent and sensible people in literary issues whom I have personally known." (Onetti's text was included by Jorge Lafforgue in *Nueva narrativa latinoamericana 2*, Buenos Aires: Paidós, 1972, p. 386.)

lustrous streets. The more unpleasant they are, the less people there are on the streets. I sleep a lot and I am getting cured. I do nothing but kill ants. The Tana says hello, says let's see if it's true that you're coming. Regarding the little things that you sent to me (your letter was not closed properly; the postman didn't understand shit. He must think that I'm gay or that I traffic in women's legs), I'll tell you:

First—The stocking has wrinkles like a fish, more than a silk stocking it looks like a skin full of scales, or better yet a support hose to hold in varicose veins (maybe that's what it's for: how many broads with varicose veins are there in Buenos Aires? Suppose there are 100,000. Think: ten pesos per pair).

Second—The story on the other hand is first class: the only thing against it is that it seems a little forced. I want to tell you, couldn't you find a twist for it that sounded less like St. Petersburg? (the whore and the anarchist, oh my God, when are you going to make up your mind to read Proust?). In any case, I like it; of course, the set-up is strong, etc. But that was foreseeable, coming from you, since you are our spiritual Bernabé Ferreyra.

Third—It occurs to me that you will never understand that you must separate literature from money. To imagine that literature is a specialty, a profession, seems to me inaccurate. Everyone is a writer. The writer does not exist, everyone in the world is a writer, everyone knows how to write. When one writes a letter (this, any) that too is literature. I would say even more: when one converses, when one narrates an anecdote, one makes literature, it is always the same thing. There are people who have never written in their lives and all of a sudden they write a masterpiece. The others are professionals, they write a book per year and publish trash to live off of it (if they can); as if it were fair that they got paid to write their filth. It is the same thing that happens with your invention of the stockings: do you think that someone is going to want to buy that kind of fish belly? Why? Why do you invest time, money, etc? If you worked on the stockings for the sake of it, to entertain yourself, it would be understandable. They are something beautiful, with good looks (I have the sample that you sent me on the table): they seem made from human skin, one touches them and they have a rubbery texture, sanguinary. There you have it: something that has no purpose, which is a pure creation, a fascinating and evil object that can be used for whatever one wants: to disguise oneself, to lock oneself up with it in the bathroom and do dirty things, or (it would be the best) to force one's wife to walk around in these stockings, with high heels and topless. But to sell them? To make them to earn money? The same happens with literature: the profession of the writer does not exist, stop screwing around already. Nobody writes because they like it or because they are given money, they write because...well, you'd know. I await you.

Kostia.

That letter was the response to a letter of Arlt's, which reads as follows:[14]

Buenos Aires, April 12

Dear Kostia:

I have not gone by there because I have been constantly occupied with this business of the stockings, since we want to come out commercially during the first days of winter. And we are going to come out with them. I enclose a piece torn off of a stocking treated with my method. You will realize that once the glaze is removed from the rubber (they will soon deliver to me a rubber that is neither glazed or textured, like this one), the matter is perfect. They will have to wear my stockings or go without stockings in the winter. There are no alternatives. To write to you of the trials and tribulations that I have performed to date is to write a novel. Just to tell you, through successive trials and tribulations I have managed to replace an aluminum leg that costs $100 with a wooden leg coated with chrome lead that costs $15. It's fantastic. I have had to invent everything, and it was not possible without tribulations and trials. Write me to tell me what impression this piece that I have sent produces in you. It can be washed with hot water. It will warm our legs in winter because its internal temperature will counterbalance the external temperature.

---

14   Roberto Arlt, *Correspondence*, Op. cit., p. 132.

Put a piece of paper with writing underneath it and you will be able to read it. So that you will try it (ha, ha), I am sending you the draft of a story which I have been writing (I first thought of it for the theater). It's a matter about the anarchists. See what you think of it and when I go to see you we'll talk. I'm fairly run-down from all the work I have. The novel is stuck not because it isn't working (I think about it all day) but because I do not have time to write a story like that. When the stockings are on the street and selling and the money starts to roll in then they will see who Arlt is. I wrote this story half by force because they asked me for it at *El Hogar* (they pay me $1 per page. More than Gálvez) and I got a $25 advance. Do you know what it's like to create on demand and at a certain amount per line? I do not believe that you nor anyone in this country knows what this infernal torment is. But this is the profession I chose, even before having written half a page, before knowing what the hell I was good for. You are in my thoughts. And I embrace you, brother, my dear.

Roberto.

PS. I will go see you without fail on Holy Week. (Speaking of Holy Week, listen to this story: Marcos Rodríguez, Spanish anarchist, condemned to life imprisonment. He refuses to have his shackles removed during Holy Week so as to look more like Christ, his Savior. Before, he went into churches and fired his revolver at the crucifixes in the middle of Mass.)

These two letters, which confirm the existence of a story written by Arlt in those days, gave me, besides, the clue as to where to begin the investigation. Keeping in mind that Arlt's letter was sent on April 12, it is clear that the story was written before this date, that is to say, toward the end of March or the beginning of April. From this, several questions arose: Arlt died in June; if the story had been in large part paid for and he needed the money, why did he not turn in a version to *El Hogar*? There were two possibilities: absorbed by the invention of the stockings he did not find the time to correct and turn in the story. Otherwise, one must think that in his meeting with Kostia (Holy Week in 1942 fell between April 22 and 25) some problems emerged with respect to the story and Arlt decided to rewrite it, or even not to publish it. In any case: had the story been preserved? To unveil this unknown it was necessary to locate Kostia. I did not have a way to reach him directly, so I went to see Pascual Nacaratti, Arlt's partner, as we have seen, in the project of the stockings; he was the person who visited him most often in those months in 1942.

What Nacaratti told me, sitting before a table on a sidewalk cafe on Carlos Pellegrini, was more or less this:

That in fact Kostia was an old friend of Arlt's. A person who exercised a large influence over him. Arlt thought in all seriousness and said to whomever wanted to listen to him, that the only writer with talent in the country was Kostia. He had memorized a poem of Kostia's which he (Arlt) had had had published in the magazine *Claridad*.[15]

---

[15]   The poem appeared in the magazine *Claridad*, VI, 24, August, 1941, accompanied by a brief introduction written by Roberto Arlt: "This beautiful poem belongs to a writer totally and voluntarily unpublished named Saúl Kostia. In the judgment of this writer, we are dealing with the best contemporary Argentine poet. R.A." This is the poem:

> Blindly tied
> to sadness and to wine
> I read books written by me, lackluster
> memories, poems staggering
> and rancid photographs
> faces set in the closed night.
> I watch the erroneous zigzagging line
> all of me encircled by sadness
> and by the light — the light
> that can no longer be serenely contemplated
> the flaming light from my head
> and those flashes of sluggishness
> upon the very foundation of all my words
> bound to sadness, and to wine
> and to the blows of black wind
> that push my poetry into obscurity.
> All of me I see like a death
> dying more at thirty years of daybreaks
> and nights, knowing, above all else,
> that there is an automobile parked at the door
> of my exposed house
> and there is an indifferent, patient,
> foolish chauffeur
> who will drive me toward Death.

"He is a poet," Arlt said. "We are simple laborers of literature. With the death of Lugones, you, Kostia, are the only poet we have left." Kostia would burst out laughing.

"Suppose I'm Balzac," Arlt would say to him. "But you are Mallarmé."

"No, I'm not Mayarmé," Kostia would say, imitating Arlt's accent. "I'm Lautremont. Is that okay with you?"

"Perfect, brother." Arlt would say.

"At that time," Nacaratti tells me, "Kostia lived in Adrogué and claimed to be an anarchist, a metaphysical poet. He spent the day reading Bakunin, reading Eliot. A guy with a lot of talent, but totally squandered. I have not seen another madman like him; when Arlt spoke to him about the business of the stockings, he proposed that they install a model sanitarium together for tuberculosis patients, copying the one that Thomas Mann describes in *The Magic Mountain*. They fought constantly but they liked each other very much. During that time, Arlt would always go to visit him in Adrogué; he stayed entire days listening to him talk. I remember one time that we were rehearsing *Cruel Saverio* and they both showed up. We went to dinner at the Hispano and at a certain point we started talking about crimes, about criminal cases. The matter took us to sexual offenses. Arlt told in great detail the story of a man in Germany who had disemboweled a fifteen-year-old virgin, and had then drawn a heart with his name and the name of the girl on the window with blood. 'That's love,' Arlt said. Kostia decided to take the stance that in a case like that the murderer should receive the same punishment. Arlt was saying that sexual deviants were modern saints because they mixed sex with death, those kind of things. As the conversation continued, I started to realize that there was a growing tension between them, and a tendency of Kostia's to ridicule Arlt's ideas. They were talking about literature and every time Kostia named *The Seven Madmen*, he pretended to make a

---

Thus, among unpublished books
and nascent books
among photographs and bottles
and friends disappeared underground,
hearing the clamor of the world in flames I await
the ending of an era.

mistake. 'Hey,' Kostia would say to him. 'For example, in *The Seven Who Were Hanged.*' He pestered him about Andreyev. All of a sudden, Arlt, who had a box of matches in his hand, threw it in Kostia's direction and hit him in the face. Kostia picked up the box with complete calm and started to light the tablecloth on fire. Before we realized it everything was a huge mess: the table had started to burn while Arlt and Kostia were throwing punches at each other in the middle of the restaurant. Suddenly Arlt let out a kind of scream, let go, and we heard him run toward the street. I remember that Kostia remained motionless, erect, his eyes shining, his face of steel, looking into the air, and said: 'I'm going to get that little madman, acting like Raskolnikov.'

"I tell you they fought, but they liked each other very much. All of us, not just Arlt, were sure that Kostia was going to be a great writer, but he fell behind, he fell behind; now he's totally deteriorated, he lives in a boarding house near Tribunales. Go see him, if you want, on my behalf. He is always in the bar *Ramos*, you'll find him there for sure, every night."

"And the story I was telling you about, do you remember anything about that?" I asked him.

"It's difficult: Arlt was always recounting projects which, later, he didn't write. You say that they paid him an advance, now the truth is I don't remember, it seems strange to me that Arlt would not have published it if they had bought it. Of course maybe it was all lies. He spent his life inventing novels that were about to come out, but which he had never written."

3

Kostia was a fat man, asthmatic, who breathed with a heavy gasping. He was sitting against a table in the back of the *Ramos*, surrounded by glasses of beer next to a woman with a low-cut, light blue dress, and a thin man with a worn out and feverish appearance. Kostia spoke as if he were preaching, and at every instant he dried his face with a wrinkled, dirty handkerchief. I settled in at the bar and watched them through the mirror that ran behind the counter.

"So you have to always ask yourself, at life's worst moment: am I sincere? You will say: And if others do not understand that I am sincere? What do you care about others? One makes a mistake when one has to make a mistake. Not a minute sooner nor a minute later. Or what do you think? That you are one of those North American multimillionaires who first sell newspapers, then they sell charcoal, then are owners of a circus, pimps, car salesmen, until all of a sudden a fortune finds them? Those men become multimillionaires because they wanted to be one. But think of all they have risked in order to make it. Do you understand?" Kostia was saying. "There is a phrase by Goethe, regarding this condition, which sums it all up. It says: 'You have put me in this labyrinth, you will get me out of it.' That's what I was saying."

Kostia stopped to breathe, passed the dirty handkerchief across his neck, and buried his face in the mug of beer. The woman with yellow hair and moist eyes was watching him, smoking, leaning against the wall with an air of boredom.

"Do you understand?" Kostia said, seeking out the eyes of the man sitting across from him.

"Yes," the man said. "You're completely right."

"Of course," Kostia said. "Of course I'm right."

"Let's go, Kostia," the woman said. "I'm sick of being here."

"In a moment, sweetheart," Kostia said. "These forces are only revealed when the thing of, 'You have put me in this labyrinth, you will get me out of it,' must happen. The voices of these forces must be listened to. They will drag you, perhaps, to perform absurd actions. It doesn't matter. You carry them out. What can it hurt? And it's clear! Everything costs on this earth. Life doesn't give anything for free, absolutely. Everything must be bought with pounds of flesh and blood," Kostia said, while the woman yawned, looking at the lights of Corrientes.

At that moment I approached the table. I told him that I came on behalf of Nacaratti, that I was working on Roberto Arlt, that I was looking for some facts and he could help me, etc. I preferred not to talk about "Luba" at first.

"Arlt?" he said, choking. "Why don't they leave the poor guy alone? What do you do? Are you a critic? Are you writing a book about him? God. I can already imagine. The crisis of 1930, psychological realism. What do you want me to tell you? Why don't you sit down?" he said, encompassing the table with a gesture. "She's Luisa, the gentleman's name is Octavio."

The woman nodded with a languid attitude, and the man whose name was Octavio took the opportunity to excuse himself for having to leave.

"You're leaving already?" Kostia said.

"Yes," the man, who seemed troubled or drowsy, said.

"Okay," Kostia said. "But don't forget what I told you."

"No," the man said. "Good, until another day then."

"One thing," Kostia said. "Can you lend me a thousand pesos?"

The man jumped; he seemed to wrinkle up, while starting to search his pockets. He took out two crumpled bills of five hundred and handed them to him.

"Don't lose track of Goethe," Kostia said. "To be able to leave the labyrinth, first one must get lost. Do you understand?"

"Yes," the man said, and looked at me with the face of someone who is suffering. "A pleasure. I'll be leaving."

"Go right ahead," Kostia said. "But don't forget what I told you."

The man started moving away down the hallway; he turned his face back to smile, timidly.

"That guy is really a poor wretch," Kostia said, and raised an arm to call the waiter. "Do you drink beer?"

"Kostia," the woman said, "when already?"

"Hold on," he said. "I'm talking with the gentleman. Do me a favor, don't be a drag."

Without answering the woman got up and headed off toward the bathroom. She wore black fishnet stockings and a short dress that made her seem younger than she was.

"So you're after Arlt. What are you looking for? Anecdotes? I can already imagine: the poor, sincere youngster, tenacious, a little rough but full of talent. The little madman, the brave one who reached the third grade and went off on his own. Is that what you want? Let's see…. He liked the haze coming off of the river because it looked like gas to him, he'd dream that all the dumb-asses in the city would become intoxicated. He liked to ride the trolley; he'd buy a round trip ticket and stay on for the whole route. He wanted to set up a school for novelists to teach how to write poorly, the only antidote for this country of poor writers. He liked married women with dumb-ass faces and whores with innocent faces. One time he spent a whole night with a street walker and didn't go to bed with her because he only had a bill of 500 pesos and he couldn't get himself to ask her for change. What do you want? Anecdotes?"

"I have been told that Arlt was with you, for one week, in April of 1942. I am gathering certain facts about the last months of his life."

"He was, yes, he came to escape, he was always taking off, always wanting to find something, who knows what the fuck it was."

At that moment the woman came back from the bathroom; she had touched up her face and her skin glowed under the violet light of the bar.

"Kostia," she said as soon as she sat down. "It's eleven o'clock."

"In a moment," he said. "He came to my house, yes, he spent a week memorizing Henry James. He wanted to write like that but something else would come out. I don't have anecdotes," Kostia said. "What do you think of him?"

"That he was a great writer."

"Don't screw around, will you? What are you going to tell me? That he was the voice of the middle class? Do you know on whose behalf Arlt spoke? For Edgar Sue, for Rocambole, for those guys. He read like a madman: everything in the Tor translations. Do you follow? Wretched steed, young groom: that was great literature for him. And he was right. Read 'The Failed Writer': that's the best thing Roberto Arlt wrote in his whole life. The story of a guy who can't write anything original, who steals without realizing it; that's how all the writers are in this country, that's how literature is here. Everything is false, falsifications of falsifications. Arlt realized that he had to write about that, in it up to his throat. Look," he said, "do one thing: read 'The Failed Writer.' The guy who can't write if he doesn't copy, if he doesn't falsify, if he doesn't steal: there you have a portrait of the Argentine writer. Do you think it's wrong? But it's not wrong, it's very good: one writes from where one can read. Dostoyevsky through the Spanish translators. Do you know why Arlt was brilliant? Because he realized that there was a style there. Then the dumbshits say he wrote poorly."

Kostia too, like everyone in this country, had a theory about Roberto Arlt. I let him talk and bought him beers; it was not his opinions I was looking for. I was looking for a story of Arlt's, and as Kostia talked I was becoming convinced that this fat guy with a red and blue striped shirt knew something about it. Finally, when he finished explaining his ideas about Argentine literature, about plagiarism and falsification, I started talking about the notebook, about the novel Arlt had been trying to write.

"Of course he was writing a novel: he was always writing. At that time he wanted to turn *The Idiot* around. He was going to write the story of a guy who becomes pure because he only thinks about money. 'If they offer me 100,000 pesos and I refuse them then I'm not a human being.' That was the theory, more or less. Metaphysics reversed: the economic crime as a road to saintliness. St. Augustine combined with Otto Bemberg."

"In any case, he was unable to finish it."

"No, and do you know why? Look at the paradox: he couldn't write it because he wanted to make money, first he wanted to become a millionaire with that stupid thing about the stockings."

Kostia was getting more and more drunk. The woman was falling asleep, leaning against the wall, a mask of tedium on her poorly-painted face.

"Now, in the notebook, inside, there was a letter," I tell him. "A letter of yours. This one, see?"

He put on a pair of round glasses, without a frame, which dug into the flesh of his face.

"Is it mine?" Kostia said, holding the letter with both hands. "Poorly written, really."

"You talk about a story. A story he had written that later, for some reason, he didn't publish."

He took off his glasses; it was as if his face became thinner.

"And?" he said.

"I think that you must know where it is, if it exists."

"A story. This woman has fallen asleep. Luisa, what are you doing?" He raised his face and looked at me, smiling. "You don't say?"

She woke up, startled.

"Let's go, Kostia," she said.

"You know very well what I'm talking about. If you find it and bring it to me, or tell me what I can do to find it, I'll pay you whatever you ask."

"Yes, we're going," he said. "So you're snooping around for the madman's scraps of papers. I can imagine. You know, I'm going to confess something to you: if I had been Max Brod, I would've published *The Castle*[16] under my name."

---

[16] The story of the relationship between Kafka and Max Brod is well known: at the moment of his death, Kafka orders his friend to burn all of his manuscripts, that is to say, that he destroy *The Castle*, *The Trial*, etc., as if they had never been written. An ambiguous gesture, it should be said that this demand is the last great Kafkaesque story. Max Brod finds himself submerged under the same feeling of guilt and postponement typical of the texts he must destroy. He is forced to choose: betray his friend or betray literature? Contradicting loyalties, double laws that place him—as we see—in Kafka's classical space. However, it is not too daring to think that the great doubt (and in this, too, Kostia is somewhat correct), the great temptation for Max Brod was not whether to publish the texts or burn them. In the issue of this double obedience I might think that the answer to the enigma was in the request itself: if Kafka had truly wished to destroy his manuscripts, he would have burned them himself. It is also not too daring to think that another doubt besieged Max Brod at some point. The doubt was (must have been) this: "Nobody—except me, expect Kafka who has died—knows of the existence of these writings. Then: To publish them with Kafka's name or to sign them and make them seem like they are mine? These texts are already no one's: they are not the writer's who did not want them. They are no one's." Immortality, fame, or the simple document of an executioner, of a gentle and humble assistant who dedicates his life to the greater glory of an intimate friend, but an unknown writer? The reverse of Herostratus (who fascinated Kafka), Max Brod's choice ennobles him but at the same time—by a strange paradox, again, typical of Kafka—it annihilates him. Would a Max Brod who usurps the fame of the deceased and who at the moment of his death reveals to someone (to another executioner, to another Max Brod) the secret ownership of those texts not have better pleased (might we not think that that is what he wanted) the distant and perverse genius of Franz Kafka?

(It will be said that I am departing from the objective of this report. That is not so at all. The fact that in presenting an unpublished text by Roberto Arlt I found myself forced to use the form of a story, the fact that Arlt's story is read inside of a book of stories that appears with my name, that is to say: the fact that it was not possible for me to publish that text—as it had been my intention to do—independently, preceded by a simple introductory essay, proves— it will be seen—that in some fashion I have been subjected to the same test as Max Brod.)

"Arlt would have too."

"Arlt would have too: I don't have any doubts about that."

"But I'm not Arlt."

"Nor do I have any doubts about *that*," he said, and started to get up. "You pay for this."

"Here's my phone number," I told him. "If you find anything, call me."

I remember that I went back home thinking that Kostia was one of those typical failed writers who spend their time writing books, endlessly, all in their minds. The story of his relationship with Roberto Arlt no doubt helped him in those exercises. He must spend entire nights talking about that friendship; it could be seen that he tried to convert it into personal ownership, as if somehow Arlt belonged to him, or better yet, as if he knew Arlt's secrets. Kostia existed for Arlt, for the memory of Arlt: without him his image was erased, it was transformed into what it was, someone mediocre, a failure who entertained himself with mugs of beer and false quotations.

I had the feeling that Kostia had attempted to hide Arlt's story for all these years. I felt like the detective in a detective novel who arrives at the end of his investigation; following traces, clues, I had finally uncovered him.[17]

I was convinced that he had the story or that he knew where to find it, and when he called me a few days later, I was not surprised.

"I have the story," he said. "Come, if you want."

I went to see him in the room where he lived and throughout

---

[17]   A literary critic is always, in some way, a detective: he pursues the contours of texts, the tracks, the traces that allow him to decipher its enigma. In turn, this assimilation (in his case a bit paranoiac) of criticism with police pursuit, is present with all clarity in Arlt. On the one hand, Arlt always identifies writing with the crime, the swindle, the falsification, the theft. In this scheme, the critic appears as the police officer who might uncover the truth. Writing that is clandestine and guilty, writing that is outside the law, it is understandable that Arlt sought that his books might circulate in their own space, outside all legal control ("In any case," he writes in the prologue to *The Flamethrowers*, "as a first measure, I have resolved not to send any of my work to the literary criticism section of the newspapers. To what end? So that an emphatic gentleman, in between the nuisance of two phone calls, might dedicate himself to discovering, for the satisfaction of the honorable gentlemen, that 'The gentleman Roberto Arlt persists in his attachment to a realism of appalling taste,' etc., etc., ... No, no and no" [Op. cit., V. III, p. 1].). On the other hand, in this affair, like in all good detective novels, what is at stake is not the

the whole conversation he behaved as if he really were a character in a detective novel: one of those shady and trapped informants who are always looking for the best way to get a good deal. He admitted that he had the story but he tried to convince me that we should not publish it; he talked and argued, simply because he wanted to get more money out of me. This I realized right away; what I did not realize was that Kostia, before anything else, was a thief; or better yet, a common swindler.

Kostia lived in one of those old, sordid boarding houses that still remain in the area of Tribunales. His room was at the end of a tiled, humid hallway, near a set of stairs that led to the roof. It was a room with a high ceiling, incredibly dirty and messy. The furniture was full of books and papers, and on the wall there was a picture of Dylan Thomas stuck up with thumbtacks. He received me stretched out on the bed, barefoot, covered with a gray overcoat with frayed lapels.

"All of this is nothing more and nothing less than a complete bastardizing," he told me as he sipped gin from a bottle. "You want some papers; I have them. I'm going to give them to you because you're going to give me money; you want to use that story to distinguish yourself, and to be able to make four or five dumb comments about Arlt. For my part, I called you because I'm a bastard. I'd like that to remain clear. He didn't want to publish it, of that you can be sure. And do you know why? Because he didn't want to publish anything unless it was dirty, destroyed, full of residue, of tatters; that was literature to him. That's what he was looking for: he called it beauty and almost nothing else in the world mattered to him. He was

---

law, but money (or better yet: the law of money). For Arlt, the critics act as art administrators; their function is regulating the distribution and the sale of books on the market: to be "criticized" (uncovered) is to lose readers; in other words, not to be able to make money with literature. Once more, like the counterfeiter who makes counterfeit bills, being discovered is not a moral problem (in this case, literary), but rather an economic one.

Finally: when someone says—like Arlt—that every critic is a failed writer, does that not in fact confirm a classical myth of the detective novel, that the detective is always a frustrated criminal (or a criminal in power)? It is not by accident that Freud wrote: "The distortion of a text resembles a murder: the difficult thing is not to commit the crime, but to hide the tracks." In more than one sense, the critic is also a criminal.

an awful writer, difficult, worse than anyone, but what he was was enough for him to be the only writer that this fucking country has ever produced. He had his own idea of what writing was; one strange idea. When he started correcting he ruined, he dirtied everything. He ruined, if you look at things from the point of view of style. I mean, if you put yourself in the head of someone mediocre. Of a guy like you or like me. Do you understand? Then, what happens? You appear and you want the papers that he didn't want to publish. And I'm going to give in. I'm going to give in and you know it and that's why you're here. Now, can you tell me what this has to do with literature?" He lifted the bottle of gin again, then continued talking. "Let's pretend that I'm selling you a woman, let's pretend that I'm a pimp and that you're one too. Huh? Let's talk about money, not about feelings."

"You're the one talking about feelings."

He smiled.

"You're right. How much will you give me?"

I said a figure.

"Too little," he said.

"Let me see it."

He moved, groping along like a blind man, and handed me a stack of dirty, crumpled sheets of paper, typed, single spaced. Just skimming through them was enough for me to realize their value.

"Do you have the original?" I said.

"That's what I have; it's worth twice what you think. If you're not interested, it's the same to me."

I paid him the whole amount he asked for.

Kostia counted the money several times and then put it away under the pillow.

"Are you content, old man? Are you happy? You have the madman's scraps of papers. Sensational: you, it's clear to see, are something like a Boy Scout of literature." He rested the bottle on the floor. "And I? Do you know what I am? A son of a bitch."

The gin made him sentimental. The best thing I could do was leave.

"Listen," he said as I was about to go out the door. I turned around; stretched out on the bed, Kostia looked at me with a kind of smile: "Fuck off, and don't show up here any more."

I traveled through the city as if in a daze; I went over the pages, I read paragraphs at random. "It's a text by Arlt," I thought. "Unpublished." I was delaying the moment of sitting down to read it, I feared that I would be disillusioned, I was trapped by a strange feeling of possession, as if the text were mine and I had written it. The story was about 5,000 words long and it was among Arlt's best stuff. The set-up seemed to come out of *The Seven Madmen*. A character like Erdosain, pursued, pure, confined with a woman whom he does not know who forces him to reveal himself and to face his limits. I reread it carefully several times. I remember that I started to jot down some ideas:

(a) The impossibility of being saved and confinement: the Arltian space.

(b) The woman as a Doppelgänger and as an inverted mirror.

(c) The prostitute: the body that circulates among men. Like a story (in exchange for money).

(d) See the work of Walter Benjamin: anarchism and artistic bohemia (in *Reflections*). The brothel as the space of literature.

I went to bed late that night and sank into a deep sleep, without dreams. I had slept less than an hour when the telephone woke me up. It was Kostia. Completely drunk, he was calling from somewhere in the city; I heard the sound of music and laughter mixed with his thick voice.

"Max Brod? Do you hear me? Listen: I'll return the money to you, give me the story."

"You're crazy."

"There are ten thousand pesos missing which I just spent. I'll give you the rest."

"Why don't you stop making scenes like a child?"

"I have done many shitty things in my life, but this time I want to stop. Do you understand?"

"Don't be ridiculous, do me the favor."

"It's a mistake, Max. If he didn't want to, who the hell are we to…?"

"This story doesn't belong to anyone, not to Arlt, not to you, not to me. It's an obligation that people—"

"A what?" He started to laugh. "You really are a dumb-ass,

old man. You work on Arlt and you don't understand. He died. What are you looking for? The imperfect manuscript, to put him at the heights of the other shit-heads. To show that he wrote as if.... And on top of it I turn out to be the one who gives it to you. I had it, he died: I saved it like an imbecile. I'll return the money to you."

He continued with that story for about half an hour. I finally hung up.

Five minutes later he called again.

The voice came through closer and more dismal, as if it were lost in the music.

"You and I are thieves," he said.

I unplugged the telephone. The guy was crazy. The best thing I could do was to leave Buenos Aires for a few days, wait until he calmed down. The next morning I left notice for the mail to be forwarded to me, and I set up at a hotel in Mar del Plata. It was the middle of winter, the city was empty, I worked on preparing the publication, forgetting everything that was not the unpublished texts of Arlt. I began to write the prologue. I insisted that it entailed, obviously, a draft; that is, a text which Arlt had not been able (or had not wanted) to publish. But I also highlighted the value of "Luba," its connections with the rest of the work. After fifteen days I got a letter from Kostia. I was sitting in the lobby of the hotel—I worked at a table near the large windows facing the sea—when they handed me the correspondence. They had forwarded a letter from my mother and a large manila envelope, without a return address, to me. Inside was the money that I had paid Kostia; it was wrapped in a cutout from *El Mundo*. It was the literary page of July 3. Kostia had published Arlt's story with the title "Assumed Name: Luba," and had signed it with his own name. *Listen, Max*—he had written in the margin in chicken scrawls, clumsily imitating Arlt's handwriting—*I owe you twenty thousand (I have spent another ten thousand). Let us say that they are the disadvantages of your profession. Yours. Kostia.*

4

I went back to Buenos Aires that same night. The train crossed the dark fields and I thought that everything was like a light dream, without an exit. Had I let myself get ripped off? In principle it was my fault: to avoid any publicity I had refused to announce the discovery of an unpublished story by Arlt before the publication was ready. My work of six months destroyed by the irresponsibility of a drunk? I remember that I passed through the cars that shook in the night until I reached the dining car. In that room with formica tables and colorless lights, ceaselessly drinking awful coffee, I tried to order my thoughts. There were only three hypotheses possible:

1) Kostia really had wanted to prevent Arlt's story from being published and known. It was absurd to think that he was trying to preserve his image; in my judgment the story was among Arlt's best stories. Was one to think, then, that Arlt himself had refused—for some reason that I did not know—its being published? In that case, why did Arlt not destroy the story? Why did Kostia save it?

2) Kostia had written the story to collect the money. If we put aside the absurdity of a guy in his condition being able to write such a story in one week, the question became, why did he return the money to me? Furthermore, why did he not tell me directly that he had written the story?

3) Last hypothesis: the story was Arlt's. Kostia had— literally — stolen it from him. In that case, why did he not do it before? Why did he not publish it when no one knew of the existence of "Luba?"[18]

Lost in these questions, I was surprised to see that the train was already sinking into the glassed vault of the Plaza Constitución. At the first phone I found, without leaving the platform, I called Kostia. Amid the confusing sounds of the trains and the people that passed by me, I spoke—I screamed—to a man with a high-pitched voice. The guy did not seem to understand; finally, after an interminable silence,

---

[18] There was also another hypothesis that perhaps only now (when everything is finished) I can propose to myself: Arlt could have specifically asked Kostia to destroy the text. In that case, what secret did the story contain? If Arlt had traveled to Adrogué during Holy Week to—also—discuss "Luba," must one think that Kostia or he himself had found something in the text that prevented its publication? Anyhow, the circle is reopened: this being the case, why did Arlt not destroy it? Why did Kostia save it? Why did he publish it under his own name? Etcetera, etcetera.

I heard a woman's voice.

"Kostia isn't here," she said.

"Tell him that Ricardo Piglia called. Who's speaking?"

"The woman, Luisa," she said.

"Tell him that I'm going to have him thrown in jail."

"In jail? Who?"

"In jail, yes, for being a thief. Tell him that. He clears up the matter or I'll have him thrown in jail."

The atmosphere of euphoria that I had left behind was still floating in my house, as if the happiness of that night in which I read Arlt's story for the first time had remained on the desk and files. During my absence, Andrés Martina had been by twice trying to see me. He explained something about a storm to the doorman. "It sounds like there was a collapse," the doorman told me. "I didn't understand very well." What did I care about that guy just then? The only thing I wanted was to find Kostia. Sitting at the desk, I spent an hour going over the files; without the story, trying to publish a book of unpublished work was useless. What could I do? I remember that I went down to the street and set out to walk through the city. It was one of those mornings, full of sun, in which winter seems to clean the air; everything was clear and transparent, women walked by wrapped in furs, and the streets were calm under the light. Without realizing it I found myself in front of Kostia's boarding house. There was the dark and dismal building, the stone balconies, the blackened cupola. The doorway smelled like moisture and reheated food. I went in without ringing. Near the window, seated facing the mirror, the woman was applying make-up to her eyes.

"Where is Kostia?"

She turned around slowly. She was wearing a light-blue night gown, her straw-colored hair on her bare shoulders.

"Listen, dear, why don't you knock before you come in?"

"I'm going to have him thrown in jail."

"Oh, yes? And why?"

"Did he tell you where he was going?"

"He went out," she said.

"Would you like some advice?"

"No," she said, her arms raised to fix her hair.

"The best thing you can do is go away, leave that guy; he's a madman, a thief."

"Him? What do you know? Kostia? He's a poet," the woman said. "And the best thing you can do is get out of here because, if you don't, I'll start screaming."

When I got home it was getting dark. I had walked around the city trying to calm down; at last I had gone into a movie theater. From the middle of the empty hall I watched the images, without seeing them; I felt like someone who loses a personal object and cannot fully convince himself of it. The bluish silhouettes moved on the screen, and I went over the facts without being able to find a way out. Finally I got up in the darkness and left. I walked back home, while dusk fell, without thinking anything, having decided to get into bed and sleep until the next day. Martina was waiting for me, sitting on a chair in the entrance hall. It was like everything was going to start over again: that man there, wearing the same gray jacket, a package just like the other one, wrapped in newspaper. In the elevator he started to tell me that he had been by twice looking for me.

"I wanted to hand it to you in person," he said when we went into my apartment. "I don't know, you'll see. There was a storm the other day, the shed is so old that it half collapsed. We're going to have to demolish it, it's a pity, no? The thing is that in a corner of the lab we found this box," Martina said. "It's full of papers."

It was a metal box, one of those boxes used to keep money. Inside I found the explanation, the motive, that had made Kostia decide to publish Arlt's story with his own name. In between dust, and sticky with a rubbery substance that seemed like liquid latex, there were three one peso bills; several samples of the fabric of the starched stockings; a copy of *The Dark* by Andreyev; one sheet of canson paper covered with chemical formulas; a page from the magazine *Argentina libre* with an article entitled "The Gloom, Or Economics Reversed," which Arlt had published in those days;[19] and a pile of manuscript

---

[19] *It entails a literary critique written by Arlt and it reads as follows*: The first enormity sustained by Menasché throughout his work is that "dictatorships are the product of the madness of one individual" and not the consequence of the needs of the capitalist class that tries to search for a way out of the economic crisis at the expense of a violent subjugation of the working class. This political monstrosity (it matters little that

pages, numbered from 41 to 75, paper-clipped together—these were the pages that were missing from the notebook. Written in ink, blurry, was the (unfinished) original of "Luba."

(From the manuscript and from the typescript that Kostia had given to me, I established the final version of the story. In the "Appendix," it will be seen that I have respected the proposed variations of the text.)

---

it be festively expressed through the vehicle of a farce) occurs (second outrageous comment) in a country whose objective conditions are absolutely contrary to those required for the establishment of a dictatorship. In Tintinabulia, our author's country, it is easy sailing for businesses, the people dance, the government clerks do not collect taxes, the masses do not know the police, nor the army, and the king is good-natured. In this economic country, which ignores the battle of the classes, Menasché has a dictatorship crystallize when every student of social problems knows perfectly well that dictatorships emerge in a country when the working class, freeing itself of parliamentary illusions, wants (or there exists a possibility that it try) to take power through violence. The bourgeoisie defends itself by squashing all the institutions of class which the democratic regime tolerates. The author actually turns out to coincide, regarding political economics, with one of our greatest men from the right, Dr. Roque Luis Gondra, professor of political economics at the University of Buenos Aires. Dr. Gondra, in character with being a man from the right, detests the dissemination of political economics because it does not conceal that scientific economics allows for the discovering, behind private property, of all the shapes of the antagonism of the classes and the technique by which man is exploited in modern society. Mr. Menasché expresses himself in like manner to Dr. Gondra regarding political economics, not because he knows it, but because he ignores it; and if Menasché had not ignored political economics, his work would not have become, in virtue of its groundlessness, a display case of commonplaces of the reactionary petite bourgeoisie.

Appendix: Luba

1

He arrived too early: it was ten at night; but the grand white hall with golden chairs and mirrors along the walls was already prepared to receive the visitors. All the lights were on. In a corner, near an almost dark drawing room, sitting next to each other, three young women were speaking in a low voice. When he entered, accompanied by the madam of the house, two of them stood up and the third one remained seated.[20] She was dressed in black, her profile was simple and serene, as if she were a young virgin wrapped up in her thoughts. And this is the one he chose precisely because she pondered in silence, because she did not look at him, and because she was the only one who seemed like a virtuous woman. He had never been in a brothel and he did not know that in all of those houses, when they are well run, there are one or two women of this kind: they are always dressed in black, like nuns or young widows, their faces pale and without makeup, their expression severe; they attempt to give men the idea of innocence but when they go with them to their chambers they

---

[20] *In the manuscript there is a paragraph which was not included in the typescript copy.* It reads: The first two, with low-cut dresses, looked at him with a feigned provocative look, which was at the same time indifferent and tired; the third, who had a very tight-fitting black dress, had turned her head; her profile was simple and serene, as if she were a young virgin wrapped up in her thoughts.

show themselves to be vicious, refined, and they carry out the most perverse acts with a distant and virginal expression. These are precisely the women with whom arrogant men fall in love, always ending up obeying their whims and dragging themselves on the ground for them.

But he did not know. When she got up with an air of disgust and severity, when she looked at him with her dark eyes and showed him her pale face, he said to himself: "But her entire aspect is virtuous." This thought consoled him. But since he was accustomed, thanks to his double life, to concealing his true feelings as if he were an actor on the stage of a theater, he greeted her like an experienced man of the world, snapped his fingers, and said to the young woman with the tone of someone who has been accustomed since early in life to brothels:

"Let's see, little one, take me to your room. Where's your nest?"

She seemed surprised, raised her eyebrows:

"Already?"

He reddened, showing his beautiful teeth, answered:

"Naturally. Why should we waste any time, precious?"

"There's going to be music. We're going to dance."

"Yeah, but what is dancing? Dumb amusement. As far as the music, we'll hear it from your room."

She looked at him smiling.

"We won't hear much from there."

In the grand mirror that reached the floor the two images were clearly reflected: she, dressed in black, very pale and fragile, and he, broad-shouldered, likewise dressed in black, likewise pale. They look so striking between those white walls, inside the golden frame of the mirror, that he stops for a moment, surprised, and thinks that they resemble two fiancés: funereal, in mourning, ready for a cruel ceremony. It's as if the young woman experienced the same feeling: she too looks strangely at her own image and her partner's in the mirror.

"Some couple," she says, thoughtful.

But he does not respond and with a determined step starts walking, taking the young woman, whose tall, French heels struck the floor, with him. Like in all of those houses there is a hallway, along which can be seen small, dark chambers with their doors half-closed. Above one of those doors it says: *Luba*. They go in.

"Luba, we need wine, and, what else is there? Fruit maybe?"

"The fruit is expensive here."

"That does not matter. And the wine. Is it that you do not drink wine?"

This time, forgetting, he did not address her informally. He realizes it right away but does not want to correct the mistake: there is something in the way the woman presses herself against him that prevents him from addressing her informally, from saying foolish things to her and from acting out a comedy. She too feels something similar. After looking at him firmly, she says with a hesitant tone:

"Yes, I drink wine. Wait, I will go order it. As far as the fruit, I will tell them not to bring more than two apples and two pears. Will you have enough with that? Will that be sufficient?"

She also addresses him formally now, but in addressing him in this way there is something confusing, like a slight wavering. He wants to keep his mind blank and not to think, and he begins examining the room just one time. First he ascertains that the door can be well closed; he is satisfied: there is a key to lock the door. Then he goes to the window, opens it and looks out: too high up, on the fourth floor, it faces the patio. Then he turns on the two light switches; when the light on the ceiling is turned off, the other one, located above the bed, illuminates with a sanguine brightness, fills the room with a reddish clarity, like a fog. The bed is short and very wide; a mirror runs along the wall, duplicating the room. He has tried to think what awaits him in that bedroom, in a brothel, but his thoughts dissolve. He has gone nearly forty hours without sleeping and sleep is like a poisonous gas that clouds his body. In this place the police will not come looking for him. He will be able to spend the night, rest a little, sleep in a bed. It is hard for him to think clearly. To calm down he takes out his Browning with eight shots, examines the chambers of the cartridge cylinder. The frozen hardness of the metal makes him feel secure. He has three boxes of bullets. They will not get him alive.

When they bring the wine and the fruit and when Luba finally arrives, he closes the door.

"Good, Luba, you drink, please."

"And you?" she asks, surprised.

"I will drink later. I've been 'on a binge' for two nights in a row and I have not slept at all, I need to rest some. You drink, don't worry. And eat the fruit. Why do you drink so little?"

"If you will allow me I could return to the drawing room. They are going to play the piano."

That would not be good for him. They would talk about the strange visitor who had stayed in a room by himself.

"No. You stay with me. Let us call it a whim."

"Yes, as you'd like. As long as you pay me."

"Yes, I will pay you, but it is not just about the money. If you would like you can lay down. There is room for the two of us. But only, you take the side next to the wall. If you don't mind."

"I don't feel like sleeping. I will remain seated."

"You can read something."

"There are no books here."

"Do you want today's newspaper? Here it is. It has a few interesting things in it."

"Thank you, I don't want it."

"As you'd like."

He turns the key twice and puts it in his pocket. He does not notice the look, full of wonder, with which the woman follows his movements. That courteous conversation, so out of place in that miserable spot, where even the air is saturated with the vapors of alcohol and blasphemy, seems very simple and natural to him. Always with the same courtesy, as if he found himself with a young lady in a canoe, he asks her:

"Will you allow me to take off my jacket?"

"Take it off. You have already paid."

"And my shirt?" he asks.

Luba does not answer. What did that man want to do with her?

"Here is my wallet. There is quite a bit of money. Would you please keep it for me?"

"It would have been better to leave it at the desk. Everyone does that here."

"Oh, it's not worth it."

"Do you know at least how much money you have? There are gentlemen who do not know and then there is a big mess because..."

"I know. But it's not worth it."

The woman holds the wallet in front of her face with both hands.

"Are you a writer?"

"Me? No. Why do you ask? Do you like writers?"

"No, I don't like them."

"Why not? They are not bad people."

"Yes. They are bad people."

He lies down, leaving a spot open next to the wall, and his face distends into a kind of joyous smile.

"What are you laughing at?"

"Nothing. I am happy. Now we can talk a little. Why don't you drink?"

"I'm going to get undressed too. I'll have to be sitting a very long time."

From the bed he sees the woman undress. The milky whiteness of her broad hips seems to fill up the mirror. He looks at her round breasts with nipples surrounded by a violet halo, and a blond tuft of hair which escapes from her sex, between her legs.

"Do you like it?" the woman says, lowering her eyes toward the bronzed curls that escape from her lower abdomen.

"Yes. You are beautiful."

She rests her knee against the edge of the bed. The lateral roundness of one breast is pressed against her folded arm. She smiles at him with a dreamy expression.

"Come here, little tiger."

"No. I have told you," he says. "Sit down, please."

"Do you want to watch me? Did you come for that?"

"No, Luba. Take a seat, I am going to rest, then if you would like we can talk."

The young woman covers her body with a red robe and sits down in front of him. She smokes slowly, drinks cognac, and watches him. The light casts him in a somewhat fantastic aspect: not young, nor old, he has a bird's face and breathes heavily.

"You are beautiful, really," he says; an instant later he is completely dominated by the sleep which embraces him strongly and carries him away toward unknown regions.

For Luba, everything in him is strange and full of mystery. His black hair is cropped very close like a soldier's; under the left temple, near the eye, can be seen the half-moon of a scar.

In the drawing room the music suddenly stops, as it fills the house with whimsical sounds. Sometimes voices and laughter and the noise of glasses are heard. Luba remains immobile the whole time, smokes cigarettes, and studies the man. At one point a voice from outside comes in clearly. "All of you in a line, all of you in a line with your eyes closed." Luba switches the light off and turns on the bedside lamp which is covered with a red lampshade. He does not move. Luba hugs her knees between her arms; she remains like that for a long time, letting the cigarette burn itself out between her lips.

2

Something grave and unexpected has happened while he slept. He understands it immediately when he sees Luba, sitting in the same position, with her pink shoulders and her naked chest, her eyes distant and immobile. "She has betrayed me," he thinks. Then he observes her better and calms down. "No, she has not betrayed me, but she will betray me." Directing himself to her, he asks her brusquely:

"Okay, what then?"

Luba does not respond. She smiles with a domineering air, her eyes fix themselves malignantly on him, and she keeps her silence.[21]

"Okay, what were you saying?" he asks again.

"Me? What I am saying is that it is time already for you to get up. Enough already! You must not take advantage. This is not a shelter, dear."

---

[21]   *Crossed out, the following can be read in the manuscript*: She'd be saying to herself that she is sure that he is hers, that he will not escape from her, and that, without hurrying, she wants to take pleasure in her power. "Okay then, what is it that you were saying?" he asks again.

"Turn the other light on," he orders.

"I don't want to."

He turns it on himself. In that new light he sees Luba's black eyes, extremely wicked, her mouth tightened with hatred, her chest naked.

"What is the matter with you? Are you drunk?"

He had wanted to get his shirt but she anticipates him and throws it underneath the dresser.

"You won't have it!"

"What's that?" he says with a choked voice, and squeezes the young woman's arm like an iron clamp. Luba's face convulses.

"Let go. You're hurting me."

He releases the pressure, but does not let go of her arm.

"Be careful," he warns her with a threatening tone.

"What? Are you going to kill me, dear? Yeah? What is it that you have in your pocket? A gun? Good: why don't you shoot me? I'd like to see it…. You really have to be courageous. He comes to a woman's house and sleeps like an animal. 'You can drink,' he goes and tells me. 'I'm going to sleep.' Ah, not that. He cuts his hair, he shaves, and he thinks they won't recognize him now. No dear! We do have police. Do you want to get snatched by the police, cutie?"

She laughs, joyous, triumphant. Fearfully, he sees the evil happiness that holds the woman prisoner, a wild happiness as if she has gone mad. The idea that everything is lost, and in a way that is so stupid that he might have to kill her, commit a cruel and useless murder, fills him with horror. Pale, but controlling himself, already having decided, he looks at the woman and follows all of her motions.

"Okay then, won't you say anything?" she insists. "Has fear cut off your voice?"

He could squash that reptile body. He wouldn't even give her time to scream. He still held her by the arm; she turned her head around like a serpent. Yes, it would be easy to kill her. But, what then?

"Luba, do you know who I am?"

"Yes."[22]

---

[22] *There are two versions of this reply in the manuscript*: "Yes, you are a revolutionary pursued by the police." Written above, it says, "Yes, an anarchist."

She pronounces this word firmly, solemnly, as if she were speaking in another language.

"How do you know?"

She smiles, mockingly.

"We're not in a jungle. We know a few things."

"Admitting that it is the truth."

"That it is the truth? But let go," she says, shaking her arm. "Let me go."

He lets go of her arm and sits down; he contemplates her with an insistent and pensive look. His face is tight but conserves its expression of sadness. She sees once again something mysterious in him, as if he were full of surprises.

"Listen to me, Luba. Naturally you can ruin me, like anyone in this house could. It would be enough to scream out. But why? Because I have devoted my life to fight for the good of others. Do you understand what it means to 'devote your life'?"

"No, I don't understand," the young woman says firmly, but listens to him very attentively.

"That has been my life. My whole life. Since always. I am not interested in anything about myself: I am only interested in the happiness of mankind."

"And could you tell us why you are so good?"

"But don't you see the world? Don't you see the injustice, the pain?"

"No. I am wicked. I'm wicked," she says, with an anguished brightness in her dark eyes. "What do I care about the happiness of others? I want my happiness. Me, me: Luba. With my body, with my sagging tits, me. What do I care about others if I'm going to be always like this, always sad and suffering!"

He looks around him, full of compassion for the young woman. Everything seems sordid to him; he thinks sadly that this is life and that there are people who live among these things for years and years.

"Poor Luba," he says, going toward her.

"No."

"Poor, little one."

"No," she says, as if catching herself.

Suddenly, with a deep groan, Luba slaps him with all of her strength. He staggers, terribly pale.

"But, what do you want to make out of me? Coward, son of a bitch," she says, leaning her body. "Did you come to make fun of me, so I'd see how good you were. Tell me what you want to do with me? Oh, I am such a wretch. And you dare, to me, you dare, you the pure one, to me who has possessed all the men, all of them. Aren't you ashamed of humiliating a poor woman?"

Covering her eyes with her hands as if she wanted to bury them in the depths of her cranium, she goes toward the bed, throws herself face down, and starts to sob. He approaches her, sweetly.

"Luba."

She continues to cry.

"Luba, don't cry."

She answers something, but so quietly that he does not understand her. He sits next to her on the bed, leans his cropped head toward her, and places his hand on her shoulder.

"I can't hear you, Luba."

She spoke again, in a voice drowned in tears, softly, as if very distant.

"Don't leave yet. They might detain you. Oh, my God. My God."

3

There is a long silence. Finally Luba sits up, lowers her eyes, and starts rotating her ring methodically. He looks at the room and tries not to look at the young woman. His eyes rest on a half-full glass of cognac.

"Why don't you have a drink?"

She seems to wake up.

"What?"

"Drink a little. Why don't you have a drink?"

"I don't want to alone."

"I, unfortunately, never drink."

"That's fine, but I am not going to drink alone."

She notices the man's gaze on her naked chest and closes her robe.

"It's cold," he says.[23]

Luba responds with an outburst of laughter.

"It seems to me that there aren't any reasons to laugh."

"We better look for some reasons. You do appear, effectively, to be a writer. Does that not bother you? Writers are like you. First they show compassion and then they get angry when one does not kneel down before them as before a God. They are demanding."

"But how can you know writers? You do not read anything."

"One comes around here."

He ponders, looking at Luba. His thoughts work feverishly with almost mechanical strength and inflexibility; he is transformed into something like a hydraulic press which, as it slowly falls, breaks rocks, bends iron bars. Now, agitated, disconcerted, similar to a large locomotive that has derailed but continues moving heavily, he looks for a way out. But Luba remains silent, in no manner does she seem willing to talk.

"Luba, let's talk calmly."

"I don't want to."

"Let's make up. Give me your hand."

She pales, lightly.

"Do you want me to slap you again? One or the other: either you are an idiot or you have not been beaten enough."

She looks at him calmly and breaks out in a burst of laughter.

"You could say that it's my writer. How can I hit you? My writer says that I know how to give slaps very well, like a gentleman, while I could hit you as much as I want, without you feeling any great thing. And you should know that I have already slapped a number of men, but none of them had inspired as much pity in me as that no-good writer. When I slap him he always yells: 'Harder, 'cause I really deserve it." She stretches her hand up high and rudely, toward his

---

[23]   *Crossed out in the manuscript, it says*: in spite of the fact that it is hot in the room.

mouth. "A kiss," she says, but before he reacts, she starts to pace around the room with a fierce air, full of contempt, no longer concerned with the man who finds himself before her, as if she were dealing with an idiot or a drunk. Her excitement grows. At times it seems like the heat is suffocating her. Twice she has filled the cognac glass and emptied it.

"But you told me that you did not want to drink alone."

"It's lack of willpower, dear. Besides, I've been poisoned for a long time and if I don't drink I suffocate. This is what I have to die of." Suddenly she opens her robe, revealing once again her beading breasts, which shine under the light. "It's so hot. Why should I cover myself up? For your consideration, your modesty? Imbecile! Listen: if you want you can take your pants off. If your underwear is dirty, I'll lend you my panties. It would be so much fun." She searches in a drawer, her body tilted over it; then she straightens up, extending a black, tulle undergarment full of lace edgings and fringes to him. "Put it on, I beg you. You will put it on, no? Dear, cutie-pie…"

Choking with laughter, she stretches her hands out in a begging gesture. Then she kneels in front of him and tries to take his hands.

"Will you give me this pleasure? I beg you, my little tiger. In gratitude I will kiss your feet."

He tries to free himself of the woman.

"Stop, Luba," he says.

She looks at him from below, kneeling down, contemptuous but happy, breathing heavily.

"Come on, why don't you want to? Are you afraid? I want to see if they fit you."

He hesitates. He looks at the woman's breasts below, soft, open. It is difficult for him to talk.

"Listen, Luba, if you insist, I agree. We could turn off the lights."

"What?" she says, astounded.

"What I mean is: you are a woman and I…. We could go to bed…. Don't think that it is out of pity…. On the contrary, I myself am interested. Turn off the light, Luba, my dear."

With a confused smile he stretches his hands out toward the

woman, awkwardly.[24] Still kneeling she looks at him with endless sadness and contempt.

"What is wrong, Luba? What is wrong with you?"

She answers in a very low voice, as if speaking to herself, full of cold horror.

"How can somebody be such a son of a bitch? My God. How can somebody be such a back-stabber?"

Luba gets up slowly. She looks for a glass and fills it again. Her head is tilted over the glass and her hair grazes her face.

"So you are the good one," she says, without looking at him.

"Yes," he says. "Yes. I am the good one, so what? I am honest, while you, who are you, you wretch? What have you done with your life?"

She has raised her face, which looks like a soft and virginal mask.

"Me? I'm a whore."

They look at each other for an interminable moment, quietly.

"Tell me one thing," she says with a serene voice. "Are you going to answer me?"

"Yes," he says.

"What right do you have to be good?"

"What?"

"Yes, you heard me. What right do you have?"

"None."

"I know, you are the good one," she says, and turns her back to him. "Do you know?" she says, and remains silent for a moment, attentive to the glass of cognac, to her fingers caressing its rim. "I have been waiting for you for a long time."

"What, you are waiting for me? For me? You?"

"Yes. I have been waiting for the good one for a long time.

---

[24]   *The version that is transcribed here is the one from the manuscript. On the typescript copy, instead, it says the following*: With a confused smile he stretched his hands toward her: it was an awkward caress, of a man who has never been with woman. She let herself fall back on her heels, still kneeling, and looked at him with an endless sadness and contempt.

Everyone who comes here classifies themselves as cowards, as bastards. And they really are bastards. My writer at first assured me that he was good; then he ended up by confessing that he too was a bastard. I don't need those people."

"And then, what is it that you need?"

"You. I need you. Thank you for coming. Thank you."

"But, what is it that you are looking for?"

"I had to slap someone who was good. A legitimate good. The others, all those bastards, are not worth slapping. That's dirtying your hands. But when I slapped you I felt a lot of pleasure. I am going to kiss the hand that hit you." With a strange smile she started caressing her right hand while she kissed it. "My dear hand, you did good work today." She cradled her hand as if it were a doll and spoke to it in a soft murmur.

"What did you say?" he asks.

She raises her face and looks straight at him. It could be said that there is pity in the eyes of the prostitute, as if all of a sudden she had gotten up on a pedestal and from high above, severe and cold, looked down at a small and miserable object thrown at her feet.

"I told you: it's shameful to be good. Didn't you know?"

"No, I didn't know."

"Good, if you didn't know that, you have to learn it."

"Did you say that it was shameful to be good?"

"Yes, my little tiger, it's shameful: it's a betrayal. Does that frighten you? It's nothing. It'll pass soon, it's only the beginning that is frightening."

"And later?"

"Oh, later.... You'll see with time. You're going to stay with me and you'll see what happens later."

"What do you mean I'm going to stay with you?"

"Waking you up has not been in vain."

"You're crazy."

"That's very bad. One shouldn't say that. When truth goes toward where you are, you have to greet it with humility. You must not say, 'You're crazy.' My writer is the one who has the habit of saying that. But he's evil, while you...you're pure. I just realized it. 'What does he want to do?' I thought. 'He wants to give me his innocence.' And you? You must have thought: 'I'll give her this gift and she'll leave me alone.' How ingenuous, Holy Mary! At first I felt insulted; I thought you were doing this because you looked down at me. Then I realized that you had done it because you're convinced that you are good. You make a simple calculation: 'I'm going to sacrifice my purity and with that I will become even more pure.' It's like having a gold coin, which can be exchanged; it's eternal and it's always worth the same. You can give it to the beggars, to the poor, but at the end it always returns to your pocket. No, dear, it won't work, I know what I'm saying."

"No?"

"No. I'm not that stupid. I've already seen these kind of merchants: they pile up millions with all the injustices and then they give ten cents to the poor and they think that they've saved their soul. No dear, you have to build the church yourself. Your innocence is not worth anything; you offer it to me because you don't need it; it's worn out, full of filth. Do you have a girlfriend?"

"No."

"But if you had one, if she were waiting for you tomorrow with flowers, with kisses, with words of love, would you have offered me your innocence? Answer me."

"I don't know."

"See? Do you realize? I'm right. You would have told me: 'I'll give you my life, but don't touch my honor.' You give what has no value. No, dear: give me what is the most valuable. Let's see if you're capable of that: give me, whatever it is, without which you could not live."

"And for what reason?"

"What do you mean for what reason? It's very simple: to be shameless."

"Luba, but you, I don't know, you too..."

"Do you mean to say that I'm good too? Yes? Really? I have already heard it. But it's not true. I am prostituted, you will never know to what extent. But soon you will learn it. When you stay with me."

"But I'm not going to stay."

"Words. Truth is not afraid of words. It's like death: when it arrives, you have to receive it such as it is. Sometimes truth is terrible, I know it well."

"And your truth, Luba? What is that?"

"My truth?" she said, calm, distant. "My truth is desire."

4

The scents of perfume and hand soap can be smelled in Luba's room; a sour, humid smell. Along one of the walls there are skirts and blouses messily hanging. Those dresses stretched out on a rope along the wall, that chamber in which thousands of men have enjoyed sexual deliriums, that smell of sin which covers the entire room, that woman with her emaciated face, was all of that truth?

"Everything is so terrible, Luba."

"Yes, dear, it is always terrible to look at truth in the face."

Confusing sounds came from the drawing room, bursts of sweet music mixed in with women's laughter. Slowly, not in a hurry, he gets up and starts to dress.

"Luba," he says, "have you seen my tie?"

"Where do you want to go?"

"I'm leaving."

"You? You're leaving? Where?"

"Do you think that I don't have anywhere to go? I'm going with my people."

"With the good ones? You're going there? Then you too have tricked me."

"Give me my wallet."

The woman hands it to him, from afar, as if she did not want to touch him.

"And my watch?"

"There it is on the bedside table."

"Goodbye, Luba."

"Then you're afraid," she asks, with a calm voice.

He looks at her. She is standing, tall, with thin arms, almost like a child's, a smile on her bloodless lips.

"You're not brave?"[25]

He has taken a step toward the door.

"And I thought you were going to stay."

"What?"

"I thought you were going to stay...with me, that we were going to be together."

"What for?"

"With you everything would be different. I would work to maintain you. You wouldn't have to do anything. You could dedicate yourself, I don't know, to living.... I would take care of everything and perhaps you could write, if you like that."

"I don't like to write. Have you seen the key?"

"It's in your pocket."

He has inserted the key into the lock.

"That's okay. Leave, since you want to leave."

He holds the latch with his right hand; she is sitting on the bed, as if she were weighed down. The scene seems to coagulate.

"Goodbye, Luba."

"Goodbye."

He has opened the door. The music from the drawing room comes up the hallway. He doesn't have to do anything other than cross the threshold. But in that last minute something incomprehensible and absurd detains him. Is it madness that sometimes takes hold of the most robust and serene spirits? Or perhaps he has truly discovered, in that brothel, under the effect of that unruly music and the eyes of that woman, truth, the terrible truth of life?[26] He passes his hand slowly through his short hair and without even closing the door again, retraces his steps and sits down on the bed.

"What's wrong? Did you forget something?"

"No."

---

[25]   *After this response, crossed out in the manuscript, can be read*: How she had changed! A few moments ago she was lofty, almost terrible, now she is sad, dejected...she is a timid girl rather than a woman of the world.

[26]   *We have respected the original version. In the typescript copy, instead, it says*:...the true, the terrible truth of life, incomprehensible for everyone else? He accepts that truth without hesitations, as if it were something inexorable.

"Then, why aren't you leaving?"

And he, calm like a stone upon which life has just spit a new and terrible command, answers:

"I don't want to be pure."

She has been leaning over; now she is stretched out next to him. With the turbid smile of a man who has found what he is looking for, he puts his hand on the woman's head.

"I don't want to be pure," he repeats, as if in a dream.

5

Seized with happiness Luba starts to move excitedly all about, to undress him like a child, to undo his shoes; she caresses his hair, his knees. Suddenly, looking straight into his eyes, she exclaims, full of anguish:

"You're so pale! Have a quick drink right away. Do you feel sick? My little Pedro."

"My name is Enrique."

"It's the same. If you want I'll give you cognac. But be careful, it's very strong. You're not used to it.

"I see that soon you will learn to drink. Very good. I'm very happy with you."

Letting out short shrieks of joy, she has jumped up on his lap and covers him with kisses without giving him time to respond. This seems absurd to him, the lack of sleep seems to engulf him in a fog; he thinks he is seeing himself from very far away, as if in reality everything were occurring in the mirror that duplicates the room. He kisses her and holds her tightly against his body without letting her move, as if he wanted to make her feel his strength. Docile and joyous, she lets him.

"You're alright, you're alright," she repeats.

She seems crazy with happiness. It could be said that the small room is full of joyous women, excited, who speak ceaselessly, kiss, caress. She serves him cognac and drinks herself. Suddenly she starts.

"Do you want to eat? Are you hungry?"

"A little."

"Right away. I'll bring something immediately."

When he is alone, the feeling that everything is a nightmare is augmented. Through the door that Luba has left ajar can be heard the distant music and the murmur of the dance.

Luba returns, still agitated.

"I brought you this," she says, handing him a plate. He starts eating. "You're not going to get mad, honey? I invited the other women.... Not all, a few. I want to introduce them to my beloved. They're good girls. No one has chosen them tonight and they're alone in the drawing room. You won't get mad because I called them? Really, you won't, honey?"

The other women are already in the room making faces and giggling. They sit next to each other. There are five or six of them, almost all prematurely aged, their faces made up, their lips darkened red. Some put on modest faces; others look at the man with a calm air, greet him, shake his hand, and wait for him to serve them something to drink. They are probably about to go to sleep for they are dressed in light robes; one of them, fat, sluggish, and phlegmatic, is in her slip, revealing her thick, bare arms and her powdered chest. This one, plus another one who looks like a rabbit, with heavy rouge on their cheeks, are already completely intoxicated. The small room fills with voices, laughter, the smell of sweat and cheap perfume.

A filthy servant, wearing tails that are too short and frayed, has brought cognac; all the women greet him in unison:

"Moscardón, dear, here's your love, over here, over here."

The servant smiles with a turbid look and walks between the women, who pet and hug him.

They have begun drinking; all the women talk at the same time, they shout and they laugh. The one with the rabbit-face talks fiercely about a client who has done I don't know what dirty thing. Insults are heard that the women do not pronounce with the indifference of men, but rather highlighting them as a challenge, cynically.

At first they pay almost no attention to the man. He himself is silent. Luba, happy, is sitting next to him, on the bed, her arms around his neck. She does not drink very much but fills his glass continuously. Every once in a while she whispers in his ear:

"My dear. My treasure. Are you okay?"

He drinks a lot, but does not become intoxicated. The alcohol, instead of making him drunk, transforms his feelings little by little. It could be said that with each new glassful he hears more clearly the desperate, diabolic voice of mysterious beings.

He stays like that, with his face wide and fragile, attentive to the women who are making a racket around him. His will is affirmed in his devastated soul: he feels capable of demolishing everything and starting anew.

"Luba," he says, "we must drink."

And when she, docile and smiling, fills all the glasses, he raises his.

"One moment," he says. "I want to make a toast."

The women's voices are slowly drowned out: their devastated and turbid faces turn toward him, forming a pallid circle.

"I drink to the health of all the bastards, of everyone who is desperate. I drink to the health of all the ladies present here." The women clap and shout. He asks for quiet, waving a hand. "I drink to the health of everyone who is squashed by life. Thieves, madmen, murderers, prostitutes. I drink to the health of everyone whose soul is poisoned. I drink to Luba's health: because she has suffered."

He totters a little and empties his glass. His voice is slow but firm and clear.

"He is my beloved," Luba says proudly. "He will stay here, with me. He is virtuous, he is good, but he is staying with me."

"He can help Moscardón," one of the women says.

"Shut up, Manka, or I'll tear your eyes out," Luba says. "He is staying with me. And he was, however, virtuous."

"All of us were virtuous once," the woman with the rabbit-teeth says.

"And I have been virtuous until now."

"Shut up," Luba says. "What do you know? You have lost your honor, while he has sacrificed it. He has willfully renounced his honor; he did not want to be virtuous any longer. You cannot understand. He…he is virtuous like a baby."

"Listen to me," he says, raising his hands. "Look at my hands. I have my life here in my hands. Do you see it? My life was beautiful.

It was pure and passionate, my life. It was like a beautiful crystal glass. But, look: he throws it on the ground."

He makes an abrupt movement and the glass shatters on the floor. Everyone's eyes have turned toward the broken glass, as if they looked there for the remnants of a beautiful human life.

"Step on it," he says. "Step on it until there is nothing left."

The women have become motionless, their faces serious, like pious masks in a semicircle. An atrocious silence fills the room. Luba observes the scene like an outraged queen. Suddenly, as if she had understood everything, she throws herself like a madwoman in the middle of the women and starts to stomp on the ground, fiercely, with her heels, in an interminable, demonic dance, without music, without rhythm.

He watches her, calm and severe.

The women start to disperse in silence. They withdraw, walking backwards toward the door, and look at Luba with a saddened expression. She has stopped her dance and looks at the floor, her face livid, contorted.

He has lit a cigarette. They are alone. On the window, distantly, quivers the sound of the rain.

"I know that you are going to leave," she says, without looking at him.

"Yes, Luba," he says. "Now I know that I can leave."[27]

The woman lifts her face, open in a painful smile.

"I know. I already realized it."

"What can I do for you?" he says. "Do you need money?" He opens his wallet and spreads the bills out on the bed. "With this money, I don't know. Luba…. With this money you can go live in the country, set up a small farm and raise rabbits. You can marry a good man. A good man who gets up at dawn and has blistered hands from working the earth so much and milking the animals. You could cure him, Luba. Every night when he returns exhausted from the field, you will put oil without salt on the skin of his hands; he will hold you up

---

[27]   The version from the manuscript is interrupted here. What follows corresponds to Kostia's typescript copy.

on an altar and on Saturdays he will round up the horses to take you to town. You know, Luba? With this money you're going to start a new life, you too. It's counterfeit money, but that doesn't matter; nobody is going to tell the difference. It's perfect: it was made by the greatest counterfeiter in South America. Nobody is going to notice, and much less out in the country, you can rest assured."

Luba has sat down on the edge of the bed without touching the money, and rotates her ring, caressing the green stone with her fingertips.

"Do you hear me, Luba?"

"What are they like?"

She raises her face.

"What are they like?" she says.

"They?"

"Your friends. What are they like?"

"They are like you and like me. Like that man who is going to marry you and who awakes with the sun to milk the cows. I have realized now that they are not pure: what they do is fight so that the world can be pure and good like a newborn baby. Do you understand?"

"Yes," she says. "But tell me what they're like."

He begins to speak to her, calmly, in a low voice, like an old man who is telling the children a heroic story from the old times. And in the reddish semidarkness of the small room, which seems to grow in Luba's tame eyes, a handful of very young men pass by, dreaming a distant future, dreaming of the brotherly men who have not yet been born but are already in life like pale phantoms.

"There are women among them," he has said. "Women who cradle the revolution like a child."

"Women?" she says.

"Yes, young and caring women, brave, who defy every danger, who carry proclamations calling for general strikes...hidden against their skin, between their breasts."

Luba gets up slowly and goes up to him.

"Am I still a woman?"

"Why do you say that?"

"Then I can live like them, like those women you're speaking about." She raises her hands and rests her palms on his chest. "Tell me, will they accept me?"

"Yes, they will receive you. Why not?"

"Let's go then where they are. You will take me, isn't that true, dear? You won't be ashamed to take me? They will understand that you had to come here and they won't reproach you for it. When a man is pursued by the police, he hides wherever he can. As far as myself, I will do everything possible so that you shall not regret having accepted me."

He has become lost in his own thoughts. He thinks he hears a distant voice which says to him: "How can you doubt that this is the doctrine? For, who is going to make the social revolution if not the prostitutes, the swindlers, the wretched, the murderers, the frauds, all the bastards who suffer below without any hope? Or do you believe that the revolution will be made by the pen-pushers and the shopkeepers?"

"Do you believe in me?" she has said.

"Yes, because it is only possible to believe in those who have nothing to lose."

"And aren't you ashamed of taking me to them?"

"No, Luba, no. You are coming with me."

She hugs him once again and then releases herself.

"Wait for me," she says. "I'll get a few things together."

"Hurry. I don't want to be caught in daylight."

Luba opens a cardboard suitcase and starts to fill it with her sequin dresses and her bead necklaces; she puts away her jars with the creams and the perfumes, and finally takes down a picture hidden toward the back of the closet. She holds it in front of her eyes for a moment and then hands it to him.

"That's me," she says. "The day I took First Communion."

He looks at the yellowish image of the small girl kneeling and dressed in white tulle, raising her face toward a metal crucifix.

"That's good," he said. "Put it away and let's go."

"I'm ready," Luba says.

They start down the long hallway, which is bluish under the sickly light that falls from the ceiling. She has put on a blue coat, and the hem of her dress shows along the edges like a stain. The women stick their gray and recently-cleaned faces out the half-opened rooms and greet her with friendly smiles. In the entrance hall the violet light glows against the mirrors. A fat and squat man, shiny, his hair slicked back, dances with a tall and languid woman, dressed in light blue. On a leather sofa the servant who the women call Moscardón sleeps with his face sunk into the lapels of his tuxedo. The music sounds warm, as if it floated on the trimmings of the ten bulbs of the chandelier.

"Good-bye, Luba," the woman says, and waves a hand in the air without interrupting her dancing.

"Good-bye, María del Carmen. Good-bye, my dear," Luba says.

In the golden-framed mirror Luba and the man are two dark, fragile shadows.

When they open the door, the sweet air of the rainy night wets their faces. The city glows, quiet in the darkness. In the background, the lights of Retiro park burn like a soft, pale fire.

"Let's go, Luba," he says.

"My name is not Luba," she says, pressing the bag against her body. "My real name is Beatriz Sánchez."

Below, the arches of Leandro Alem seem to die in the haze of dawn.

Translator's Notes

Note: The following notes are presented without endnote numbers. This approach has been taken for two reasons: First, in order to avoid disrupting the flow of the stories; Second, as the reader will have noticed, "Assumed Name" contains a series of numbered footnotes. These belong to the author; they are, in fact, an integral part of the content and style of the novella. The endnotes are intended to clarify certain items with which non-South American readers may not be familiar. They are listed under the title of the story in which they appear and keyed to page and keyword(s).

Mousy Benítez Sang Boleros

50: Julio Jaramillo A singer of boleros famous in the 1950s and 60s.

The Glass Box

58: Tacuarembó The capital of the Uruguayan province of the same name, in north-central Uruguay.

62: Payadores Payadores were gaucho minstrels that impro-
vised poetic folk songs, accompanying themselves with a guitar.

62: Juan Lavalle (1797-1841) was an Argentine general who
fought under San Martín in Argentina's revolutionary war.

The Madwoman and the Story of the Crime

67: Coperas Coperas are women who receive a commission for
every drink purchased by the men whom they entertain in bars and
clubs.

68: Macarena Refers to the Virgin of the Macarena, who is
named after the famous neighborhood in Seville.

71: Entrerrianos Entrerrianos are the citizens of Entre Ríos, an
Argentine province north of Buenos Aires.

71: Lanús A working-class suburb of Buenos Aires.

Assumed Name

Homage to Roberto Arlt

91: The Furious Toy Roberto Arlt's *El juguete rabioso*, a 1926
novel, has not been translated into English. It is the story of Silvio
Astier, a young man who is fascinated by the world of crime.

92: Etchings Arlt's *Aguafuertes*, short chronicles about the city
of Buenos Aires published in the newspaper *El Mundo* between 1928
and 1993, and later collected in the volume *Aguafuertes porteñas* in
1933, have not been translated into English. Arlt continued writing
these texts until the year of his death, but they were not published
during his lifetime.

92: The Seven Madmen and *The Flamethrowers Los siete locos y Los lanzallamas* is Roberto Arlt's second novel. It was published in two parts; the former in 1929, the latter in 1931, and only *The Seven Madmen* has been translated into English to date. It is the story of Erdosain, a young man who, when he is accused of stealing money from his job (a true accusation by a relative) and is abandoned by his wife, joins a group of anarchists who a plot an utopian takeover of the country.

93: Bánfield   A working-class suburb of Buenos Aires.

96: Carlos Pellegrini (1846-1906) President of the Republic of Argentina from 1890 to 1892, and founder of the National Bank of Argentina in 1891.

108: The Failed Writer "El escritor fracasado" is a short story by Roberto Arlt, included in the collection *El jorobadito* (1933); it has not been translated into English.

109: Ushuaia   The capital of Tierra del Fuego, on the furthermost southern part of Argentina, Ushuaia is the southern most city in the world.

112: Juan Carlos Onetti   (1909-1994) Arguably the most important Uruguayan writer of this century, Onetti is the author of numerous works of fiction, including *A Brief Life* (*La vida breve*, 1950) and *The Shipyard* (*El astillero*, 1961).

113: Tana   (Or Tano) A nickname for a person from Italy, namely a Neapolitan.

113: Bernabé Ferreyra   A striker on Buenos Aires' soccer team River Plate in the 1930s. A notable scorer, famous for his strength and the power of his shots, he was known as "La Fiera" ("The Beast").

117: Leopoldo Lugones (1874-1938) The foremost modernist Argentine poet, his best-known works include the poems in *Odas seculares* (1923) and the stories in *La guerra gaucha* (1926). Very little of his work has been translated into English to date.

117: Cruel Saverio Saverio el cruel is a play written by Arlt, produced in Buenos Aires in 1936.

122: Otto Bemberg A multimillionaire, of German descent, Bemberg was the main producer of beer in Argentina.

Appendix: Luba

150: Moscardón A pet name, usually used for an importunate person, someone who is a pest or a nuisance. Moscardón literally means a botfly or a hornet.